THE MERCILESS III

ORIGINS OF EVIL

DANIELLE VEGA

RAZORBILL

AN IMPRINT OF PENGUIN RANDOM HOUSE

RAZORBILL

An Imprint of Penguin Random House
Penguin.com

alloy**entertainment**

Produced by Alloy Entertainment
1325 Avenue of the Americas
New York, NY 10019

ISBN: 9780448493527

Printed in the United States of America

1 3 5 7 9 10 8 6 4 2

Design by Liz Dresner

ORIGINS OF EVIL

PROLOGUE

*T*he blood feels warm beneath the cold metal. She shifts her body, trying to lessen the weight of the chains, but this only makes them dig deeper, bite harder, until her skin is raw. Shredded. A drop of blood winds around her wrist and splatters onto the floor next to her bare foot. It looks like a tiny flower. Red and perfect.

"Help," she whimpers, but the word sounds too small for what's happening to her.

A man laughs.

She jerks her head to the left, and then to the right, but she doesn't see him. The chair is stiff behind her back, and the chains hold her firmly in place. There are no windows in the small room, no overhead lights. It's very dark, lit only by flickering candle-light that glimmers over the objects hanging on the walls.

A blade. A spike. A chain with sharp, cutting edges.

She tries not to look at them.

A footstep sounds, and then a shadow falls over her. She hears him breathing. She presses her lips together, trying to be quiet, but a sob escapes, echoing off the wall.

"Shhh." His voice is barely a whisper. "God is listening. He wants you to be strong."

He steps away from her, and there's a sound like metal scratching on metal. He's taken something from the wall.

No. Not that. Not again. She throws her weight against the chains. She curls her toes into the floor. She twists and slides, but she can't get free. He's speaking again, telling her to be calm. To stay still. She doesn't want to stay still.

He lifts something over his head. It sounds big. Heavy.

"This will be over soon," he says.

But he's lying.

CHAPTER ONE

I stare at the phone for so long my eyesight blurs.

"Ring," I whisper. I rest my chin in my hands and wrap my fingers around my face, digging them through my tightly braided hair and directly into my scalp. "Come on. Ring."

The phone refuses. It's a useless hunk of white plastic that's so old it's almost yellow. I pick it up and the dial tone pierces my ears with a sharp beep. Not the shitty landline's fault, then. I drop the phone back onto the receiver with a little more force than necessary.

It's only the first night of the helpline, but so what? Why the hell isn't anyone calling? The people in this town need serious help, and I know everyone's heard about what I'm doing. Between weeks of Facebook posts and flyers and announcements over the school loud-speaker, there isn't a single person in this suburb who doesn't know about *Brooklyn's cute little project*. Or what-ever they call it behind my back.

I even agreed to set up the helpline in the school basement, even though there are dozens of empty class-rooms right upstairs. It smells like a toilet down here, and there aren't enough overhead lights to illuminate the long, narrow room. And the walls are all plastered with freaky motivational posters. *You have potential! Reading is winning!*

I uncap a Sharpie and doodle tiny vampire kittens all over my last Teen Helpline flyer. I came up with the idea a month ago, when a story about a teen suicide in Southaven was all over the news. People kept saying this poor girl killed herself because she didn't have any-one to talk to, which I thought was bullshit. The only helpline around here is affiliated with the community center and run by this super-conservative moms group that won't mention the word *drugs* and doesn't believe in gay people.

I'm not even kidding. They *don't believe in them.* Like they're unicorns.

Anyway, the girl who killed herself needed someone real to talk to. Like me.

I wanted to call my project the Teen Hell Line (get it? Because being a teenager is hell?), but Ms. Carey vetoed the swearing. Now I'm stuck with Teen Helpline, which is so boring. No wonder nobody's calling. Or maybe the teens in this town want to stay screwed up.

I watch the clock tick toward 8:00 PM. I'm drawing a tiny set of fangs on another kitten when the phone rings.

Finally. I grab the receiver. "Teen Helpline, this is Brooklyn."

"Hello?" a girl asks. "Is this where you call to get advice about stuff?"

"That's right," I say. The helpline is supposed to be anonymous, but this girl's voice sounds familiar. "Did you have something you wanted to talk about?"

"You can't tell anyone what I say, right?"

She's definitely someone I know. I clear my throat. *Anonymous*, I remind myself. That's the whole point.

"I have to call the police if you tell me you're in danger, but otherwise that's right. This is completely anonymous."

Some of the tension leaves my chest. All those YouTube videos I watched to prepare must've helped, because my voice was calm and warm—totally professional.

"Okay." The girl pauses. Takes a deep breath. "Because I was wondering whether you knew if, um, I could get pregnant . . ."

I flip my notebook to the page where I jotted the

phone numbers for Planned Parenthood and a couple of counseling centers.

". . . from a toilet seat," the girl finishes.

My fingers go still. "Damn it. Deirdre, is that you?"

The girl on the other end of the line dissolves into a fit of laughter.

"You left one of your flyers at the shop," Deirdre explains. She works at Liquid Courage, this tiny tattoo parlor in downtown Friend. I can picture her there now, a couple of ballpoints sticking out of her frizzy hair, bare feet kicked up on the front desk. "Sorry, but I couldn't help myself. It's been slow as shit tonight."

She laughs again, releasing a snort that makes her sound like a donkey. Normally I'd give her shit about it, but right now I'm too pissed.

"You're tying up the line," I snap. "Someone with a real problem might be trying to call."

"Oh, please. Has anyone called? Like, at all?"

I grind my teeth together. "That doesn't mean nobody *will*. The whole point is to be here. It's not a popularity contest."

"Whatever. It's just a little advice line."

I bite back a bitchy comment. Deirdre and I are friends because we both understand that life is shit. The difference is that Deirdre thinks it's funny, and I want to fix it.

"Just because you'd see a house on fire and watch it burn doesn't mean some of us wouldn't try to help," I say.

"Don't start with me," Deirdre moans. "Ditch the holier-than-thou attitude and come have a drink at Liquid. Santos already left, so we'll have the place to ourselves."

Santos is a bad decision I made last summer. I cringe at the memory. "What about Ollie?" I ask. Ollie and Santos own the tattoo parlor together. "Ollie said he'd fire your ass if he caught you drinking at work again."

"*Please.* Ollie loves me. You still grounded?"

She says "grounded" like someone else might say "contagious." Deirdre graduated from high school last year, moved into her own place, and immediately forgot what it was like to have parents. She acts like being sixteen and living at home are rare, horrible diseases. School hasn't been the same without her, but we still hang out almost every day.

"Officially, I'm grounded until I learn that 'two wrongs don't make a right,'" I say, cradling the phone against my shoulder and making air quotes she can't see. "Unofficially, I'm betting they'll give in by tomorrow night. Dad's been complaining that I 'sigh too loudly' when he's grading papers, so I know he's ready to get rid of me."

"They didn't buy that stealing lipstick was a political statement?"

Last week, I got caught pocketing a tube of Rich Girl Red from Drugmart. It's bullshit, because the people who own Drugmart are sexist assholes who don't sell day-after contraceptives and refuse to give their employees health insurance. They *deserve* to be stolen from. Unfortunately, my parents didn't see it that way. Neither did the Drugmart security guards. They tell me I'm lucky they let me off with just a warning.

"Look, Deirdre, I really gotta go. Someone—"

"Yeah, yeah," Deirdre says. "Call me when the wardens let you out of your cell, okay?"

"Will do."

I drop the phone onto its crusty receiver and lean back in my chair, sighing. The motivational poster directly in front of me shows a boy in a thick sweater running down the path toward a quaint-looking school building. He's holding a report card, and he has this wide, vacant smile plastered across his face. The slogan reads: *Always do your best!*

I slide my chair over, angling my body so I'm not facing him anymore. He seems smug.

The clock ticks from the wall. *Tick. Tick. Tick.* The helpline is open until eight. Someone still has thirteen minutes to call. I can handle thirteen more minutes.

A spider creeps across the floor, legs twitching. I lean over in my chair and crush him beneath the sole of my combat boot.

Tick. Tick. Tick.

Five minutes left. I color my nails in with my Sharpie. A phone beeps—I jump, drawing a thick line across my pinkie—but it's just my cell, not the helpline phone. I dig it out of my pocket and check the screen.

It's a text from my mom: **Pick up milk on your way home?**

OK, I type back. I shove the phone back into my pocket and then lick my thumb and try to scrub the Sharpie line off my pinkie.

Tick. Tick. Tick.

Two minutes left. I stand and start shoving my books and notes back into my backpack. It used to be my mom's, from when she was in high school, and it's falling apart. The only things holding the threadbare fabric together are the faded patches ironed onto it. There's an alien face with black, almond-shaped eyes, a rainbow-colored peace sign, and a logo for Pearl Jam.

I pull my jacket on, catching one last glance of the *Always do your best!* boy as I fumble with the buttons. The photograph looks like it was taken in the fifties. It's black and white, and the edges have all turned brown and gone dog-eared. I do the math in my head. If the boy had been fourteen when the photo was taken, and the photo is sixty-five years old, he'd be in his late seventies now. Or dead.

"See you later, dead boy," I say as I head for the door. I start up the creaky wooden stairs.

A high-pitched ringing sounds behind me.

I groan. It's probably Deirdre again, or another prank call. I drop my backpack on the floor and hurry back to the phone.

"Teen Helpline," I answer, balancing the receiver between my chin and shoulder. "This is Brooklyn."

Silence. I sink down into my chair. "Deirdre, come on, I have to—"

A ragged inhale interrupts me. I stop talking. That doesn't sound like Deirdre. I press my lips together, my heart thudding in my chest. It's a real caller. My *first* real caller.

I read online that you're supposed to be patient with the kids who call in. Not everyone wants to talk about what's bothering them right away. Sometimes people just want to hear another voice and know there's someone else out there.

"You don't have to say anything if you don't want to," I say, doing my best to keep my voice soft and soothing. "But I'm here to listen when you're ready. Do you think you can tell me your name?"

I wait for a beat, staring at the black smudge on the floor that used to be a spider. One of its legs twitches— then goes still. The caller doesn't answer me, but I hear slow, shallow breathing, so I know she's there.

"Okay, you don't have to tell me your name," I say. The breathing stops. "Can you—"

A loud, desperate sob echoes from the receiver. I'm stunned into silence, my heart beating so hard it makes my chest ache.

"Hello?" I try again. "Are you safe?"

The crying dies down a little. "Help," a girl's voice whispers. "He's . . . he's hurting me."

I grip the phone with both hands. "Who's hurting you? Where are you?"

There's a beat of silence. I press my ear hard into the receiver, listening for breath, crying, *anything*. There's a *click* and the dial tone blares.

She's gone.

I don't remember standing, but I'm on my feet and my chair has toppled to the floor. I'm still holding the phone. The dial tone echoes off the concrete walls of the basement.

Calm down, I tell myself, placing the phone back on its hook. This could still be another prank. I left flyers for the helpline all over Friend, and there are more assholes in this stupid suburb than anywhere else in Mississippi. I pick my chair up and sit down again, thinking.

She said someone was hurting her. It didn't sound like a prank. It sounded like a real girl in trouble.

I dial 911 with trembling fingers.

"Friend Police Department, what's your emergency?" The woman's voice is clipped and efficient, with a hint of the familiar Mississippi accent I've worked so hard to lose.

"I work at a teen helpline," I explain. "I just got a really weird call . . ."

I repeat what the girl said to the operator. For a second, I hear only the clacking of computer keys. Then, "Thanks for the information, miss. We've traced the call, and the address we're showing is 4723 North Maple Avenue. Does that sound right?"

Her voice has the rote tone of someone verifying information I already have. I clear my throat. "I . . . I don't know. It's anonymous."

There's a pause. "Of course. We'll dispatch an officer right away."

I wait for her to say more, but she doesn't. A second later, I'm greeted with another sharp dial tone.

I hang up the phone and drop my head into my hands, my palms slick with sweat. I feel like I could run ten miles. Like I could scale the side of a building. But all I can really do is sit here. It's up to the cops to help now.

I swallow, my heartbeat slowing. Friend isn't exactly known for its stellar police force. The cops here spend most of their time trying to catch underage kids sneaking into dive bars, and yelling at homeless people for loitering outside of gas stations. Friend is very safe. Which is just another way of saying boring.

I drum my fingers against the table. *4723 North Maple Avenue.* That's just a few blocks away from the school.

The police station is all the way across town. Friend isn't big, but it'll take them at least ten minutes to wind through the narrow, twisting streets.

I think about the fear in the girl's voice, her desperate sob. *He's hurting me.* She might not have ten minutes. I could hop on my bike and be there in two minutes, easy.

I grab my backpack and race up the stairs.

CHAPTER TWO

A church looms ahead, its windows dark.

I slow my bike to a stop, dropping one foot to the ground to keep my balance. I'd been expecting a run-down house with boarded-up windows and broken beer bottles in the yard. Not a *church*. But the address painted across the front of the curb reads *4723*, so I know it's the right place.

It's bigger than a church should be, more like a fancy community center than a place of worship. Neatly trimmed bushes and trees surround the two-story brick building, their leaves already browning in the October chill. An angled roof cuts into the sky, red shingles blocking the crescent moon. There are no stained glass windows or gothic arches, no statues of Jesus or the Virgin Mary. A slender gold cross hangs over the front doors, the words *Christ First Church* emblazoned below.

A police cruiser idles in front of the building, exhaust billowing from its tailpipe. Its siren lights swirl, flashing red and blue, but the sound is off. That was quick. After a moment, a cop climbs out, grunting as he adjusts the nightstick hanging from his belt.

My lip curls. *This* is the guy they sent? He looks like his mother still cuts his hair, and his uniform practically hangs off his skinny frame.

The cop takes his time lurching up the stairs to the main entrance. I'm wearing all black—black cut-off shorts, black band T-shirt, black combat boots—but my bike's painted bright pink with flecks of black, the seat covered in peeling green duct tape. Like a watermelon. Not exactly stealthy, but I wasn't planning on an espionage mission. I ease my bike into the shadows as the cop tugs a flashlight from his belt and switches it on. A white beam cuts through the darkness.

"Hello?" He aims the flashlight beam through the glass doors of the church. "Anyone in there?"

No one answers. He peeks into the glass of the front doors, tugs at the handle. It's locked. The cop turns the flashlight off and pulls a walkie-talkie from his belt. "No one here," he calls back to his cruiser. "Probably just some asshole kids messing around."

He walks back down the stairs and climbs into his car, where I can see the silhouette of his partner waiting for him. A second later, the car pulls away.

I watch his headlights disappear down the street in disbelief. *That's it?* A girl calls for help, and all the cops do is look through a window for two seconds?

Anger burns inside of me. This is everything that's wrong with the world. You call on someone whose entire job description is to protect the city, and they act like it's a goddamn burden. I briefly consider chasing after the junior cop's car and throwing rocks at the taillights, but that wouldn't help this girl, either. I don't know why I bothered with the cops in the first place. I should know better.

I hurry up the steps to Christ First. I try the door to make sure it's locked. It is. I press my face to the cold glass and look inside.

I don't know what I expected to find. A clue, maybe. Or something that might tell me whether the call was a real cry for help. But all I see is a dark, empty hallway.

I walk down the side of the building and around to the back, pulling on side exits and knocking on windows. No luck. There's no one here. I make it all the way around to the front entrance and sigh, my breath fogging the glass. I'm no better than the cop.

* * *

I push through my own front door ten minutes later, dumping my backpack on the floor next to the life-size statue of a praying Buddha that Mom bought during her college semester in Thailand. My leg itches. I scratch it with the toe of my boot, and the skin burns. I glance down.

My calf is covered in dried blood, and a gnarly looking cut twists over the skin. My bike chain must've sliced it open when I raced to the church. I lean over and touch the edge of the cut with my finger, cringing as fresh blood oozes out. It's deep.

"Crap." I swipe a tissue from one of the boxes Mom leaves all over the house and mop up the blood. Standing, I call out, "I'm home!"

"Kitchen," my dad yells back. I duck through our musty, book-filled study and down the long, winding hall to the back of the house.

Most people in the suburban hell town of Friend, Mississippi, prefer shiny, cookie-cutter houses with soaring ceilings, pristine white walls, and five-car garages. Not my family. Our house looks like the Addams Family mansion. The rooms are all cramped, with funky light fixtures and strange nooks built into the walls. There's a narrow cupboard next to our stove that's only big enough for tiny spice jars, and the ceiling in my bedroom is angled so sharply that it's almost impossible not to smack your head against it. At night, the whole house groans and creaks, like it wants to come alive.

Dad stands over the stove in the kitchen, stirring something in a large silver pot. He must've just gotten home, because he's still in his professor clothes—tweed jacket, Goodwill sweater, and the bright green New Balance tennis shoes he wears with everything even though they match nothing. He looks like the original hipster, only he's not doing it ironically.

"Taste this?" he asks, dipping a spoon into the pot and holding it out for me. "I can't tell if it needs more salt."

I take the spoon. It's his famous tomato sauce with sausage and homemade meatballs. The recipe was passed down from my great-great-great-grandmother, who supposedly emigrated from Italy with only the clothes on her back and a recipe for meatballs stuffed down her shirt. It's the only thing Dad knows how to cook.

"It needs red pepper," I say, leaning against the counter. The cut on my leg stings.

"Told you," Mom says, walking into the kitchen behind me. She sets a basket down on the counter and starts filling it with bread. "Did you get the milk?"

"Forgot. Sorry."

Mom flashes me an annoyed look, all the more effective because of her messy hair and dirt-smeared T-shirt. Mom has the worst black thumb of anyone I've ever met, but she's convinced herself she's going to be a master gardener despite killing every plant she touches. You gotta be impressed with her ability for self-delusion.

She hands me the bread basket. "Set the table."

I take the bread into the dining room. Dad's teaching assistant, Elijah, sits at the table, crouched over a daunting stack of ungraded papers. Elijah's a sophomore this year. He's tall and skinny, with longish, brown hair that he pulls into a bun at the back of his head and a tattoo of an avocado just below the crook of his elbow.

Dad teaches religious studies at Magnolia State College, this tiny liberal arts school just outside the city limits. Friend might be the devil's asshole, but Magnolia State makes the place slightly more interesting. Everyone who goes there is a total freak.

Elijah nods at me without looking up. "Yo." He's wearing a T-shirt that reads BOYCOTT DRISCOLL'S BERRIES.

"What's with the berries?" I ask, plopping the bread onto the table and sliding into a chair.

"Driscoll pays their farmworkers only six dollars a day." Elijah turns a page in the essay he's reading and circles something with a red pen. "It's inhumane."

I nab a slice of bread and rip it in two. "And you're going to make it all better with a *T-shirt?*"

Elijah cocks an eyebrow, eyes still on the paper he's grading. "You got a better idea?"

"Burn their factory farms to the ground. That would send a message."

Elijah finally looks up. His eyes are almost black, like two pools of oil. "Not exactly environmentally friendly. Or legal."

"At least you'd be showing them you mean business. Has anyone even noticed your little boycott?"

Mom walks into the dining room. "Elijah, are you staying for dinner?" she asks, placing a salad on the table.

"Not tonight, Mrs. Stephens," Elijah says. "I'm library-bound. Early morning lit test tomorrow."

"You can't study on an empty stomach," she points out.

"The library has vending machines."

"You don't want to try my famous tomato sauce?" Dad asks. He's carrying a heaping bowl of pasta sauce in one hand and a stack of plates in the other. Elijah eyes the bowl hungrily.

"I really have to get to the library," he says, starting to collect his things.

"Next time, then," Dad says, handing me a dish. "Brooklyn, how did the helpline go tonight? Get any callers?"

I shrug, staring down at the bread in my hands. "Someone called, but she hung up before I could do anything."

Dad spoons some pasta onto my plate. "At least you took the call and listened."

"She needed someone to do more than listen," I say, poking a meatball with my fork. "You didn't hear her— she was totally freaked out. She said, 'He's hurting me,' and the only thing I could do was call the cops, and they didn't even *do* anything—"

"How do you know what the cops did?" Mom interrupts. Suddenly she's in full mom mode—eyes narrowed, mouth pinched. *Shit.*

I clear my throat. "Well, I don't *know*, exactly—"

"Brooklyn, please tell me that you didn't go looking for that girl," Dad says. His voice makes all the hair on my arms stand on end. It always gets real low and quiet when he's pissed. It's worse than if he just yelled, like Mom does.

I glance over at Elijah for help, but he's staring very hard at the floor.

"She said someone was hurting her," I say. "What was I supposed to do?"

Mom closes her eyes, pinching the bridge of her nose. "You were supposed to trust the police to handle the situation. How many times do we have to go over this with you?"

"You can't fix everyone yourself," Dad adds. "And you're grounded—"

"So I should just stop trying, right?" I snap. "Let the grown-ups handle everything even though, guess what, they never actually do anything!"

Mom slaps her hand against the table. "You could get hurt, damn it!"

"Maybe I don't care about getting hurt!"

Elijah is backing toward the door now, a pink tint to his cheeks. "I should get going," he says. "I'll, um, see you in class tomorrow, Mr. S."

"I'll walk you out," I say, pushing back my chair.

"No worries—" I shoot Elijah a look, and he snaps his mouth shut, swallowing. "I mean, thank you."

I follow him to the front door. My parents start arguing as soon as we're out of the room, but they keep their voices down.

"I didn't know your dad could get so pissed," Elijah says once we reach the entryway. He glances over his shoulder, like he thinks my parents might hear us from all the way at the back of the house. "I thought his eyes were going to pop out of his head."

"Yeah, well, I bring out the worst in him," I say, leaning against the wall. Dad's bronzed platter of John the Baptist's severed head sits on the table behind me. It was a gag gift from one of his students a few years ago, but Dad insists on displaying it near the front door and acting like it's fine china.

"Sorry I have to bail," Elijah says. "For the record, it sounds like you did the right thing tonight. Going after that girl, I mean."

"Really?" I say. "You don't agree with my parents?"

"Nah. They're scared you'll get hurt, which I get. But that's not a good enough reason not to help."

Elijah tightens his bun, but his dark hair is short enough that half of it has fallen around his neck.

"Why do you bother with that?" I ask to change the subject. "It's the skimpiest man-bun ever."

"Sloan likes it."

Sloan is Elijah's girlfriend. I met her once. She was crying like a baby as she raced out of my dad's office. She wears steel-toed combat boots that look like they were made for stomping on kittens, and won't shave her pits for political reasons, but as soon as she gets a B on a midterm she becomes a sobbing mess. She seemed a little high-strung for someone as laid-back as Elijah, but it's not really my business who he dates.

"Sloan owns an I LOVE KALE T-shirt," I point out. "I wouldn't trust her taste."

"Hey, kale is delicious," Elijah says, laughing. He pulls the front door open but turns to face me again before stepping outside. He's so tall and lean that I have to stretch my neck back to look up at him. "You should give your parents a break," Elijah says, tightening his grip on his messenger bag. "You're lucky you have people to worry about you."

"They don't realize how tough I am."

Elijah shrugs and steps outside, the door swinging shut behind him. I'm about to head back to the dining room and face my parents' wrath when he turns back, catching the door with one hand.

"Hey, maybe that's the problem," he says, poking his head back inside. "You expect everyone to be as strong as you are, and you can't deal when they aren't."

"That's not a problem," I point out. Elijah shrugs.

"Depends on how you look at it."

CHAPTER THREE

I'm standing in our dining room. Alone. The only light comes
from two long candlesticks in the middle of the table. White-
orange flames flicker on twin wicks. The platter holding John the
Baptist's head has been turned into a centerpiece, and it glints
in the low candlelight.

Someone starts to cry. I turn, but there's nobody in the shadows behind me.

I move toward the table, the severed head. It's facing the
opposite wall. Light reflects off the bronzed strands of his hair
and the bones jutting out of his decapitated neck. I walk to the
other side, so I can see his face.

It's not John the Baptist anymore. It's a girl I don't recognize, tears running down her cheeks. Her eyes flutter open.

Help, *she whispers. Her teeth and tongue are coated in blood.* He's hurting—

I jerk awake, knocking my geometry textbook to the floor. The kid sitting next to me snickers. I pretend to scratch my nose so I can flip him off.

"Nice of you to join us, Brooklyn," Mr. Huston says from the front of the classroom. "We're discussing the difference between acute and obtuse angles. Would you like to weigh in?"

"Um . . . acute angles are adorable?" I ask. More kids laugh. Mr. Huston shakes his head and turns to write something on the chalkboard.

I pick my book up off the floor and flip through the pages, but I can't figure out which chapter we're discussing. The words and numbers all blur together.

I uncap my Sharpie, sketching loopy circles on a page about how to calculate the area of a rhombus. I focus on the black ink bleeding through the paper to keep myself from replaying the dream.

The clock ticks from the wall above the door. *Tick. Tick. Tick.*

The sound burrows into my brain. *Time's up,* it seems to say. *You can't help her. You can't help anyone.* I grit my teeth and jam the felt marker into the page, ruining the tip.

I've already come up with a hundred different ways I

could've broken into that church, and it hasn't even been a full twenty-four hours. I've imagined myself picking the lock with a hairpin, or throwing a rock through the window, or calling in a bomb threat.

But I didn't do any of those things. A girl called to tell me that someone was hurting her, and I just walked away.

I cast a glance at the front of the room to make sure Mr. Huston is occupied and then slide my cell out of my pocket, tilting my textbook to block my hands from view. I pull up a browser and type *Christ First* into the search bar. I click on the first link—Christ First Church of Friend, Mississippi.

Their mobile site is pretty slick. Big-box churches like Christ First probably rake in tons of dough by guilting their patrons into tithing each month. I scroll past dozens of high-res photos of smiling teenagers and their well-adjusted parents. Someone spent a lot of money trying to make Christ First seem cool. I find the youth group page and click, tapping my fingers against my desk as a photo loads. It's a girl my age, her hands lifted over her head, her eyes squeezed shut in prayer.

"Oh shit," I whisper, lifting my hand to my mouth. The girl in the photo is *Riley Howard*. The same Riley Howard sitting two desks in front of me.

I peer over the top of my textbook at Riley's perfectly blown-out chestnut-colored curls. She scribbles something onto a piece of paper and passes it to the girl behind her, who's fiddling with a tiny gold cross hanging from her neck.

Riley is the embodiment of everything that's wrong with Friend, Mississippi. Glossy and perfect on the outside, rotten on the inside. She's completely incapable of being authentic. Every word out of her mouth is a lie.

She was my next-door neighbor all through junior high. She hangs with a crew of basic bitches now, but we used to be like sisters—I have the old friendship necklace to prove it. The summer before freshman year, she and her family moved into one of the mini mansions in the rich part of town, and Riley turned into a Barbie doll. She started spending two hours a day curling her hair, and wasting insane amounts of money on jeans that were probably sewn together by underpaid children in Bangladesh. We barely saw each other at all that summer. I walked past her lunch table on the first day of high school, but every seat was already filled. She didn't invite me to sit down, and I could hear her new friends laughing at me as I stalked away.

I was actually relieved. If I had to spend the rest of the school year listening to her talk about shoes or mani pedis, I'm pretty sure I would have strangled her in her sleep. That's when Deirdre came into my life and everything got much better.

I glance at the photo on my cell screen again. I didn't even know Riley went to Christ First.

The bell rings. Riley balls up a piece of paper and tosses it toward the trash can. It misses and rolls across the ground, but she doesn't seem to notice. Or care.

"Riley, wait up," I call. Riley turns at the sound of my voice. I weave through the desks after her.

"Brooklyn! Hi!" She stretches out the word "hi" so that it has two syllables. *Hiyeee*. It's the kind of fake greeting you give to someone you don't actually want to talk to.

"Hiyeee," I say, mimicking her. The corner of Riley's mouth twitches, but she covers it by pressing her lips together. It's the same smile I've seen her use at school bake sales and class officer elections. It would look pious, except her eyes stay empty. Like she's a doll.

"What do you want?" she asks.

"I heard you go to that Christ First place? What's their deal?"

"Oh gosh, Brooklyn! Are you finally ready to accept Jesus Christ into your heart?" She forces her fake smile even wider, her nose wrinkling as she scans my outfit. "You might want to change first. Wouldn't want you to burst into flame."

"Some of us can take the heat."

"Whatever." The fake cheeriness has drained from

her voice. "Why do you suddenly give a shit about my church?"

"I met a guy last weekend who says he goes there," I lie. "Does the youth group have anything coming up? I was thinking of swinging by."

Riley's smile twists. "Can't think of anything. Sorry!"

She turns on her heel and stalks out of the room without another look back, flipping a curl over her shoulder as she goes.

I slip my phone out of my pocket and check out the Christ First website again. After 2.5 seconds of poking around, I locate a long list of public events hosted by the youth group—including a Battle of the Bands tonight at seven.

I imagine the look of horror on Riley's face when she catches me there, and it's all I can do not to laugh out loud. I click out of the website, find Deirdre's number, and shoot her a text.

Not grounded anymore. Want to go to a concert?

I wait for Deirdre on the sidewalk outside Christ First while Jesus-loving zombie-teens swarm around me on their way through the main doors. They could be mirror images of Riley, with their designer clothes and good hair and wide, fake smiles.

Two guys walk past me, wearing the exact same

loose-fitting jeans and Affliction T-shirts. If either of them has a single original thought in their brains, I'll donate my entire college savings to Christ First.

Music plays inside. I can't hear the actual words, but bass pulses through the sidewalk beneath my feet, making the soles of my boots vibrate. I pull out my cell and start dialing Deirdre's number. If she ditches I'm going to—

"Bitch! Over here!"

Deirdre's voice booms over the rest of the crowd. I pocket the phone and look around. I spot Deirdre's hair first. She has the kind of thick, black curls that grow out instead of down and stick out from her head at all angles. She bounces over to me, wearing high-waisted, mint-green, cut-off jean shorts, knee-high athletic socks, and a cropped tank that says WEASEL on it. Inexplicably.

"Look at the guys here," she says, too loudly. "Don't you want to take them home and teach them how to pray?"

"No one here is going to believe that you know how to pray," I say, grabbing her by the arm. "Besides. We're on a mission."

I told Deirdre all about my mystery caller already, so she knows why we're here, but she still pouts.

"We're always on a mission," she says. "Just once, I wish our mission could just be 'go to concert—flirt with boys.'"

"Next time," I promise.

We follow the music through the winding halls of Christ First, past giant framed photographs, all showing groups of people posing next to half-built houses, or holding baby ducks on oil-covered beaches, or digging through piles of hurricane debris.

"These people really like volunteer work," Deirdre says.

"I guess," I say, frowning. Something about the people in the photos bothers me. They all stare at the camera with the same strange, plastic smiles plastered across their faces, their eyes wide and vacant.

I shake the weird feeling as Deirdre and I wander into an auditorium the size of a basketball court. A table filled with chips and soda stands near the door, and someone's passing around glow sticks and necklaces. The neon greens and oranges and pinks flicker beneath a spinning disco ball hanging from the ceiling.

I take it all in, stunned. When I first saw the words *Battle of the Bands* on the Christ First website, I pictured wooden pews and hand-holding and "Kumbaya" played on an acoustic guitar. Christ First didn't get that memo. The teens in here are packed shoulder-to-shoulder, dancing to an actual rock band playing on an actual stage. I don't see Riley in the crowd yet.

I nudge Deirdre with my elbow. "Let's check out the band."

She nods, and we weave through the crowd and make our way up to the stage.

A short, thin girl stands behind the microphone, swaying under the bright lights. She wears a wide-legged jumpsuit and chunky platform boots. Silver thread sparkles from her black hair.

"You can't be sure he'll want you back when you return," she sings, her voice a deep, throaty tremble. *"But I'm sure . . ."*

The guitarist comes in with a jagged riff that makes the hair on my arms stand straight up.

"These guys don't suck!" Deirdre shouts over the music.

I nod, rising to my tiptoes to catch a glimpse of the guitarist. I can barely see past the bobbing heads in front of me, but I spot blond hair and the corner of a white T-shirt—

"Brooklyn, *hiyeee.*"

Shit. I try to keep the grimace from my face as I turn. Riley stands behind me, flanked by two of her vapid, perfect-looking minions. I recognize Alexis Donahue immediately. She used to hang with Riley and me back in junior high. Riley was always making fun of her thick Southern accent, but unlike me Alexis managed to make the jump to high school friend. I glance at the girl to Riley's left. I don't recognize her.

"Hey," I say, nodding at them. Alexis flashes me a vacant smile and flips her blond, Disney-princess hair over one shoulder.

"It's *so* cool that you came," Riley says, like she actually invited me, fake smile already firmly in place. She and Alexis exchange a look they think I don't see, and then Riley's eyes flick over to Deirdre. "Who's your friend?"

"We've met before, Riley," Deirdre says. "Remember? We were in P.E. together last year? I let you have a tampon that time?"

"I think you have me confused with someone else," Riley says. She nods at the girl to her left, the one I don't recognize. "This is Grace. She's new."

"Hey," Grace says, waving. She has dark skin and thick, black braids, her eyelids covered in glittery gold. One glance at her tells me that she's way too cool for this town. "I just moved here from Chicago."

"I'm sorry," I say. Deirdre snickers. Riley flashes Deirdre a look.

The band onstage releases a final, earsplitting wave of sound, and the crowd around us erupts with cheers.

"Thank you," the guitarist says into the microphone. I'm too short to see his face over the backs of people's heads, but his voice is deep and scratchy. "We're Fishers of Men. Before we take off, I want to remind you all that donations from tonight's show go to benefit Disciples of Jesus, Christ First's summer missionary fund."

A dozen kids weave through the crowd, waving baskets over their heads. Almost everyone in the room starts pulling out cash. Ten- and twenty-dollar bills pass between their fingers. I stare, shocked. I did a fundraiser for the Red Cross once, and in more than two months, I barely managed to raise $100. I try to calculate how much money gets shoved into baskets in just a few minutes, and quickly lose count. Even Riley slides a twenty-dollar bill from her pocket and drops it into a passing basket.

"Stay blessed," the guitarist says. The girl in front of me shifts to the left, and I can finally see the stage and catch a glimpse of his face. Tanned skin, thick blond hair, and a smile that's too wicked for church. I officially upgrade him from guitarist to hot guitarist.

"Damn," Deirdre whispers in my ear. "Why didn't we become Christians sooner?"

"Because you're Jewish," I whisper back. "And I don't believe in God."

"Details," she mutters.

"Now," the hot guitarist continues, "it's my pleasure to introduce our fearless leader, and my dad, Pastor Joe Whitman."

"He's the pastor's son," Deirdre hisses to me. "That's hot."

A man wearing a baseball cap and jeans jogs onto the stage. He has a full head of pure white hair, although he can't be more than forty years old, and the deeply tanned skin of a game show host. He smiles, showing off dozens of sparkling, white teeth.

Pastor Joe lifts a hand, and the crowd quiets.

"Thanks for that introduction, Gavin. Everyone, let's put our hands together for my talented son and his band, Fishers of Men!" Pastor Joe smiles even wider. The lights glare off his smile. The crowd cheers and whistles.

"Before I bring the next band to the stage, I want to take a moment to talk to you all about Jesus," Pastor Joe says.

The room falls silent. Like they've been placed under a spell. I glance at Deirdre. She makes her hand into a gun and pretends to shoot herself in the mouth.

"Jesus isn't a name you hear every day. He's not popular in schools or on television. He doesn't play football." This must be a joke, because a few people in the crowd laugh. Pastor Joe's smile widens. "No, Jesus was just a poor carpenter with a message that changed the world.

"Some of you out there might be thinking—but what does that have to do with *my* life? How can Jesus help *me*? All I can say to you is *try it*. Accept Christ into your heart and see how your world changes."

More clapping. Someone near the back of the room wolf-whistles.

Crazy, Deirdre mouths to me. I stifle a laugh.

"I can see a few of you are still skeptical of what Christ can do in your life," Pastor Joe continues. I glance back to the stage and find his eyes trained on me. A chill goes down my spine. Did he catch us laughing?

"I have a story for those skeptics. See, I wasn't always a believer, either. When I was younger, I didn't trust anything I couldn't prove. I spent a lot of years of my life arguing that if God was real, he'd show himself to us. He wouldn't expect us to believe in something we couldn't see or touch.

"After my wife died, I went through some dark times. I was lonely. I had a new baby at home, but I didn't know how to be a dad. It was like there was a hole in my chest, and no matter where I looked I couldn't find anything to fill it. I turned to drugs and alcohol, but they just made that hole bigger.

"One day, when I was driving home from some bar, a little dog ran out in front of my car. But I'd had a few beers that night, and I couldn't slow down . . ."

Deirdre grabs my arm. "Oh no. Not the puppy!"

"My car shook when it slammed into that dog's body. I stopped driving, but I couldn't make myself get out. I knew I'd killed that poor dog, and my shame was like a physical thing weighing me down. It was like a presence in the car with me. I felt it so strongly that I actually looked into the rearview mirror to make sure there wasn't someone else in the car. And that's when I saw it."

Pastor Joe is quiet for a moment, but nobody speaks.

"There was a shadow in the backseat, watching me. And I realized that the shadow was my sin. It was my shame and my anger and my fear. And if I stayed in the car with it, that shadow would take over my life. So I opened the door, and I got out of the car, and I knelt beside that little dog. He wasn't breathing too well, and I was pretty sure he wouldn't make it. But I felt something then, something I can't really explain. It was like God had put his hand on me. And right then, I knew what I was supposed to do. I placed my own hands on that dog, and I felt God's energy pour through me and into him. I've never felt anything like it before. And wouldn't you know it, that dog stood right up and ran away."

The crowd around us cheers and claps. Deirdre leans over to me. "You know God is *dog* spelled backward?"

"Who in this room feels a shadow in their life? Who needs to rededicate themselves to Christ right now?" Pastor Joe asks. The clapping grows louder. "All right then! Come on up to the front. Right here. We're going to pray for you."

A trickle of people make their way to the front of the room. They crouch before the stage, and Pastor Joe closes his eyes and raises one hand over his head.

"Heavenly Father," he says in a rumbling voice, "I want to thank you for putting your hands on us tonight. We are just so blessed to have you in our lives, showing us the path to righteousness."

I look around. Every single person in the auditorium has their head bowed, their eyes closed, and both hands lifted toward the ceiling. A girl near the back sways in place, so filled with the Holy Spirit that she can't stand still.

I glance at Deirdre. She shrugs and lifts a hand over her head. I do the same. It feels pretty dumb.

"Jesus," Pastor Joe continues, "I pray that you shine your light down on us and watch out for every single soul in this room tonight, especially those of us who've stumbled, those who need you now more than ever before. Praise his name."

"Praise his name," the rest of the room echoes. There must be hundreds of people in here, but their voices merge together as one.

Pastor Joe ends the prayer with an "amen," and then heads down the short staircase to the side of the stage. He's immediately surrounded by a large group of teens. I watch him smile and give them high fives—and then I get it. The prayer was weird because it didn't feel like we were praying to Jesus.

It felt like we were praying to Pastor Joe.

CHAPTER FOUR

"Charismatic leader? *Check.* Mean girl who wants to keep you away? *Check.* Call for help from someone on the inside? *Check.*" Deirdre swipes a Sprite off the refreshments table and cracks it open. "Girl, I believe we have a cult."

I glance over my shoulder to make sure no one heard her. We're wallflowering it on the far end of the auditorium, next to the refreshments table and the exits.

I lean against the wall next to Deirdre, scanning the crowd. "All of Christianity is basically a cult."

"True." Deirdre slurps soda fizz from the top of the can. "So what's your plan?"

I rub my eyes with two fingers. The plan was to check this place out and see whether anyone looked like a total creeper or my caller, but I'm starting to see the flaw. It's church. *Everyone* looks like a potential perv or victim.

"Just keep an eye out for anything that seems weird," I say.

"Like that chick?" Deirdre points, and I follow her finger to a girl standing alone in the opposite corner swaying to the music with her eyes shut. A single tear falls down her cheek.

"I think God is putting his hand on her, right now," I say, and Deirdre snorts with laughter.

"What was *up* with that speech? Do you think Cult Leader Joe really believes a *shadow* made him hit some dog with his car? I think he hit it because he was driving drunk. Like an asshole."

"*Exuseme?*" someone says.

I flinch and turn. A heavyset boy stands behind me.

"What did you say?" I ask. The boy nods at the table I'm standing in front of. "*Exuseme?*" he says again, and this time I notice the wires weaving across his teeth, holding his jaw shut. He tries to move his lips around the words, but it doesn't do any good. He sounds like he's chewing gravel.

I shuffle to the side, and the boy steps forward.

"*Dankyou,*" he says. Specks of blood dot his teeth and

lips. I cringe, wondering if the wires hurt. He plucks a soda from the table and goes back to his group of friends.

"We need to be more careful," I mutter to Deirdre, motioning to another group of guys edging closer to the refreshments table. "That kid almost heard us talking. We don't want the villagers to chase us out with torches and pitchforks."

Deirdre mimes zipping her lips shut, and I go back to checking out the crowd. For all our jokes about this place being a glorified cult, the kids don't seem all that different from the students at my school. They're boring. Preppy. Bland. If one of them is hiding some deep dark secret, I'm not going to figure it out by watching from the soda table.

I study a group of girls in the middle of the auditorium. One of them steps away from her friends to check a message on her cell phone. Her perfect suburban-girl mask slips as she reads it. Another girl leans over to say something to her, and the mask slides back over her features. She smiles like nothing's wrong, shoving the phone back into her pocket.

"That was weird, right?" I ask, nodding at the girls.

Deirdre shrugs. "I don't know. They look pretty normal."

"That girl totally just hid that text message from her friends. And whatever it said pissed her off."

"Yeah, but it could have been anything. Like, what if

her mom texted to say she needed to be home an hour early? And look, now she's laughing again."

I glance back at the group, and Deirdre's right. The girl is bent over her friend's shoulder, laughing so hard she can't seem to breathe. Crap. I snatch a Coke from the table, scanning the crowd for anyone else. There's a girl in a fight with her boyfriend—she storms off; he follows her. Another girl looks sad, and another looks angry. The rest dance and talk. They all seem to be having fun, but any one of them could be faking. There's no way to know for sure.

"You're doing this wrong," Deirdre says. "You'll never find your mystery caller by standing in the corner. You need to go talk to people."

"What am I supposed to say? 'Hi, my name is Brooklyn, did you call my helpline two days ago sobbing about some crazy man trying to hurt you?'" I turn my body to face hers and lean my side against the wall.

Deirdre flicks the tab on her soda can with one finger. "That's not what I meant. You need to find someone who goes here to show you around. Like a tour guide."

"If you're talking about Riley, I'd rather—"

Deirdre's eyes flick to something over my shoulder. "Not Riley."

She winks and then pushes me—hard. I stumble into whoever's behind me. A dozen hideous swear words flash through my head, but I clench my mouth shut to keep from saying them out loud. Because church.

I turn to face whoever I just fell on, and—oh. It's the guitarist. The *hot* guitarist who is also the creepy cult leader's *hot* son. He somehow manages to smile without moving his mouth—his eyes crinkle, and his expression brightens, and his whole face grows warmer.

"You okay?" he asks, lowering a hand to my shoulder to steady me. With that tan skin and mess of curly, golden hair, he looks kind of like a cherub. A sexy cherub.

"Fine. I just"—I shoot Deirdre a dirty look—"tripped."

"Yeah, it's pretty crowded." Hot Guitarist runs a hand back through his messy curls. He's wearing a thin white T-shirt that's still sweaty from his set. When he lifts his hand, I see a strip of skin between his shirt and the waistband of his jeans. My cheeks burn.

"You're new, right?" he asks. His voice doesn't match up with his angel face. It's deep and gravelly. "I don't think I've seen you around before."

Deirdre loops an arm over my shoulder before I can answer. "Brooklyn runs a teen helpline. She's looking for a girl who called in a few days ago."

I clench my teeth. *"Deirdre."*

"What? I don't get all the cloak-and-dagger stuff. You can't help this girl if you can't find her." Deirdre turns back to the guitarist. "Can you think of anyone who might have called? Anyone who might need help?"

Hot Guitarist frowns, his eyes moving from me to Deirdre. "Look, it's cool of you guys to try and help, but that doesn't sound like Christ First. We're all about fellowship here. Kind of like a big family. If someone had a problem, they'd talk to my dad, or bring it up in youth group."

Deirdre looks at me, eyebrows lifted. "You did say it could've been a prank."

I press my lips together, still staring at the laces on my boots. I'm not sure yet. The fear in that girl's voice seemed real. If it was a prank, it was a convincing one.

"Big family, huh?" I lift my head and look around the auditorium. "Does that mean you know everyone here?"

Hot Guitarist leans past me to grab a soda. "Everyone except you," he says. "I'm Gavin, by the way."

"Deirdre," Deirdre says, pointing at her WEASEL T-shirt. "And you've already met Brooklyn."

Gavin flashes us a smile. "It's a pleasure, ladies."

I blink and look away. I came here for a reason, and that reason had nothing to do with developing a crush on the pastor's son.

I point to the girl who'd been fighting with her boyfriend earlier. They both just wandered back into the room, and the girl's face is all pink, like she's been crying.

"What's their deal?" I ask.

"A test?" Gavin grins for real now, revealing a mouthful of straight white teeth. "Okay, let's see." He turns toward the couple, his brow screwed in concentration. "That's Claire and Logan. They've been dating since freshman year, but he just got accepted into this Jesuit volunteer program in Seattle. I think she's pissed because it means they're probably going to break up."

"All right," I say, mentally crossing Claire off my list of potential mystery callers. "What about her?"

I nod at the girl who seemed so upset after getting a text message. She has bushy brown hair pulled back into a braid, and thick black glasses. Very future-librarian-slash-cat-lady.

"That's Abby," Gavin says. "She's cool, but pretty shy. I actually went to her mom's wedding last year. Her step-brother's kind of a jerk, though. I don't think they get along."

I glance at Deirdre.

"He's not, like, a *violent* jerk," Gavin cuts in, reading my mind. "He's more of a cocky drinks-too-many-protein-shakes type who really likes listening to himself talk about CrossFit. And Abby's already told us all about him at youth group. If she was having issues, we'd know."

"Doesn't sound like your girl," Deirdre says, taking a drink of soda. I frown, itching my shin with my boot as I look for another contender.

Gavin stares down at my leg, his face twisting in concern. "Hey, you just started bleeding."

"What?" I look down. I covered the cut on my calf with

tiny, mustache-shaped bandages before I got dressed this morning. I must've re-opened it when I scratched my leg just now, because a red blotch has spread across my jeans, telling me the mustaches didn't do the trick.

"Shit!" I cover my mouth with one hand, cheeks burning. "Damn, I'm not supposed to say that in church, am I?"

"It's fine." Gavin takes my soda and sets it down on the refreshments table next to his. He grabs my hand. "I can fix it. Come with me."

The sudden skin-to-skin contact is too much. Energy pulses up my arm, electrifying my entire body. I glance at Deirdre, but she shakes her head, saying, "I'm good. See you in a few."

I make a face at her that Gavin doesn't see, and she winks. "HOTTIE," she mouths, silently, as soon as his back is turned.

Gavin leads me through a side exit, dropping my hand once we reach the hall. A restroom sign glares from the semidarkness. Gavin stops in front of a door marked LADIES.

"Wait," I say, stopping him. "I can handle it from here."

Gavin pushes the door open, his expression serious. "This is an emergency. Sit."

He nods at the counter next to the sinks. I push myself up, while he stops in front of a locked cabinet. There's an easiness to his movements that tells me he belongs here. Not in the girls' bathroom, but in every room in Christ First. I guess a pastor's kid probably treats the church like a second home.

He fishes a set of keys out of his pocket, but he doesn't unlock the cabinet. Instead he wedges one of the keys between the doors and uses it to pop the cabinet open, revealing rows of bandages, gauze, and aspirin bottles.

"The lock's been broken for years," Gavin explains, grabbing a box from one of the shelves. "I used to be on the Christ First junior soccer league, and we were always sneaking in here for Band-Aids."

I picture a tiny golden-haired Gavin chasing after a soccer ball and can't help smiling.

"Such a rebel," I say. Gavin kneels in front of me and rolls up the ripped leg of my jeans.

"That's me," he says, letting his gravelly voice go even deeper. A chill shoots up my spine. "Rotten to the core."

He grabs a paper towel off the counter and runs it under cold water. "Now, clearly, you can see that tiny mustache Band-Aids were the wrong choice here." He peels the soggy mustaches from my skin and mops up the blood with the paper towel. He touches me carefully, like my leg is something precious. His fingers are cool and soft. "This is a job for a heartier Band-Aid. You might even need gauze."

"You don't have to do this," I say, wrinkling my nose. "It's gross."

"What kind of Good Samaritan would I be if I didn't help a lady in need?" Gavin unwraps a Band-Aid and places it over the scratch, patting it down to hold it in place.

"I thought you were a rebel."

"I guess I'm both."

I wrap my hands around the side of the counter and lean forward, staring down at him. There are freckles on the back of his neck, and the top of his head is a mess of curls. The tag is sticking out of his T-shirt.

I reach out and tuck it back in, my fingers grazing the skin on his neck.

Gavin lifts his head, an unwrapped Band-Aid in one hand. His lips pull into a surprised smile. "What—"

The door bangs open, cutting him off. I look up, expecting Deirdre, but the lead singer from Gavin's band walks in.

"Oh! I'm sorry." She pushes a lock of silver-threaded black hair behind one ear, revealing three tiny diamond studs winking from her cartilage. A triangle-shaped cutout in her jumpsuit shows a glimpse of brown skin just above her belly button. Her eyes widen as she takes in the scene of blood and Band-Aids. "Is everyone okay?"

She speaks in a slow, melodic way. Like she'd rather be singing.

"Hope, perfect timing." Gavin winks at me and then looks away so quickly I almost wonder if I imagined it. "I need a nurse. Grab me another Band-Aid? This box is empty."

"That's okay," I say. "It's all bloody—"*And I want to be alone with Gavin*, I think, but Hope is already shaking her head.

"I don't get squeamish," she says. She leans over Gavin to stare at my mangled leg, resting one hand on his shoulder. Possessively. A lock of her silver-threaded hair falls against his cheek. He twitches, but doesn't brush it away.

Oh. The air around us seems suddenly thicker. Like the bathroom is about to combust. Whatever heat I'd imagined between Gavin and me is like a flickering match compared to the explosive energy between him and Hope.

I feel like I've been slapped awake. Of course the hot guitarist would be hooking up with the boho princess lead singer. It's like a hipster fairy tale.

"It's just a dumb bike injury," I mutter, staring at Hope's hand on Gavin's shoulder. Her fingernails are all painted a perfect glossy black, like a row of shiny beetles. Gold rings glitter from her knuckles. She doesn't have a single ragged cuticle.

I roll down my pants and hop off the counter. This

isn't my night. Time to find Deirdre and get the eff out of here before the hottest girl in the Christian cult realizes I was undressing her boyfriend with my mind.

"Nice meeting you," I say, slipping past Hope and Gavin. "And thanks for your help, Gavin."

I'm out the door before either of them says another word. Usually I can spot a guy with a girlfriend a mile away. But Gavin had me fooled.

The bathroom door slams open and swings shut.

"Hey, Brooklyn! Wait up."

I turn to see Gavin rushing down the hallway after me. He grins and shoves his hands into his low-slung jeans. There it is again—that flickering match of heat between us.

I clear my throat. "Yeah?"

"You left too quickly," Gavin says, brushing a stray curl behind his ear. His voice isn't as confident as it was two minutes ago. "I didn't get a chance to ask for your number."

I bite my lip to hide my look of surprise and glance at the bathroom door, half expecting Hope to come racing out of it, beetle-black fingernails ready to claw at my face. But the door stays closed. "What about Hope?"

"Hope?" Gavin looks genuinely confused. He tilts his head, and an adorable line crinkles the skin between his eyebrows. "What about her?"

"She's not your girlfriend?"

Gavin actually laughs, like this idea is ridiculous. "Brooklyn, Hope is my sister."

I open my mouth and then close it again. Now it's my turn to be confused. There's no way that *Hope*, with her glossy black hair and dark eyes, shares genes with this blue-eyed, blond-haired guitarist in front of me.

"*Adopted* sister," Gavin clarifies, seeing the look on my face. He takes a step toward me, trailing his fingers down the back of my arm. Shivers race over my skin. "Dad found her at an orphanage in South America after my mom died. I was only two when it happened, and she was the same age, so I sometimes forget the adopted part." He flashes me a mock-frown, deepening the crinkle between his eyebrows. "Why did you think she was my girlfriend?"

I roll my lip between my teeth. This new information changes what I witnessed in the bathroom. The moment breaks apart and re-forms in my head. Hope touched her brother's arm. Innocently. Like you would totally do if you've lived with someone your whole life. That energy I felt must've been their sibling bond.

"I don't know," I say, and my lips quirk into a smile. I dig my Sharpie out of my pocket and scrawl my digits onto Gavin's arm. The ink seeps into his skin. Branding him.

Gavin blows over the numbers to dry them, his breath tickling the backs of my fingers. "What're you doing now?" he asks in his low voice.

"Nothing. Why?"

"Hope sent me out here to invite you to the after party." He straightens and looks me in the eye.

Hope sent him. My smile becomes fixed.

But sisters stick their noses into their brothers' dating lives all the time. Deirdre is constantly complaining about the revolving door of blank-faced waitresses her brother brings home from his bartender job. We spent hours last month plotting how to get rid of Lacy, who pronounced *faux pas* like "fox paws."

"I could hit up a party," I say. "Lead the way."

CHAPTER FIVE

Deirdre and I pile into Riley's massive yet already packed SUV along with a slew of Christ First teens whose names I don't bother learning. I focus, instead, on the fact that Gavin's leg is pressed against mine, the warmth of his skin seeping through his jeans.

"Smells like Jesus in here," Deirdre mutters into my ear, scooting in next to me. We're four to a row now. If we were any closer I'd be sitting on Gavin's lap.

"So, Brooklyn," Hope says, leaning across her brother's lap. Strands of her long hair trail along his jeans. "What's your story? Where do you go to school?"

"Adams. Are you at Eastern?" I ask, since it's the only other public high school in Friend.

Gavin shakes his head. "Mountaincrest."

"That's the Christian prep school, right?"

"The very one," Hope says. "Dad doesn't like us to associate with the real world if he can help it. He thinks atheism is contagious."

Gavin pushes his sister off his lap. "You're making it sound like we're in a cult."

Hope rolls her eyes. "If the shoe fits . . ."

I don't look at Deirdre, but I can feel her body stiffen next to me, trying not to laugh.

"I've heard Mountaincrest has a great outreach program," I say, elbowing Deirdre to keep her from snorting.

"Yeah, we do." Gavin shifts his body toward me, his eyes brightening. "Every year they send people to different places around the world to help strengthen the community or rebuild after a natural disaster."

"Like Habitat for Humanity? Our school doesn't even collect cans for the homeless."

"Sort of. But we don't just build houses. We help set up schools and churches. Last year we started this letter-writing campaign to get some of the local hospitals to donate medical equipment."

I don't know what to say. I wanted to do Habitat for Humanity last year, but my mom thought I was too young. The program at Gavin's school makes my little helpline seem pathetic.

"That's amazing," I say.

"Yeah, I've been lucky." Gavin looks down at my hand resting on my lap, studying my Sharpied nails.

Riley turns the car off the main road, pulling into an unfinished development. The strip mall lights and cookie-cutter split-levels fade into the background, replaced by mounds of unpacked dirt and abandoned construction equipment covered in tarpaulins and plastic. All of the streetlights are dark.

Friend is full of places like this—fancy neighborhoods that smell of hope and money, started when the economy seemed steady, and abandoned when Wall Street ran off with all the cash. Some have started construction again, but this one is clearly dead. Empty, half-built houses watch us drive past, their bare beams skeletal in the darkness.

I lean forward, sticking my head between the two front seats. "Hey, Ri, where exactly are we going?"

Riley bristles at the nickname—left over from when we were kids. "Daddy owns this development. We're going to borrow one of the houses for the night."

I lean back in my seat, begrudgingly impressed. Prissy little freshman-year Riley would never have snuck in someplace she wasn't invited.

We pull up in front of a house that looks almost finished except for its streaky paint job and packed-dirt lawn. Lights flash behind the windows, telling me we're not the first to arrive. Riley cuts the ignition and throws open the car door.

"When did you start coming out here?" I ask, climbing out from the seat behind her.

"About the same time you started wearing safety pins as earrings." Her eyes travel down the length of my body, taking in my shredded jeans and the fluorescent pink bra clearly visible beneath my tank top.

"I'd dress like you, but I can never remember where you shop. Was it Talbots? Or Chico's?" I ask.

Riley releases a huffy sigh and hurries across the lawn to catch up with her friends Grace and Alexis.

"What a bitch," Hope says.

I snicker. "I thought you and Riley were friends."

"Not really. She acts like she wants to be voted Miss Teen Christian Mississippi. I guess that means buddying up to the pastor's daughter, but I find her a little . . ." Hope pauses, searching for the right word.

"Fake?" I offer.

"That's it," she says, snapping her fingers.

I study Hope's profile. Sharp, uptilted nose, full lips, black eyes. Even in the dark she looks cool and confident. I bet she wouldn't be caught dead with these people if she weren't the pastor's daughter.

Gavin climbs out of the SUV. Everyone else has already hurried inside to join the party. Gavin rests his hand against the small of my back. He could just be try-ing to direct me toward the house. Or he could be using this as an excuse to touch me.

"Come on," Hope says, heading for the porch. "Let's get a drink."

"You guys drink?" Deirdre asks.

"We're not Amish," Gavin says.

"And holy water tastes great with vodka," Hope adds.

Deirdre's eyes bug. *"What?"*

"She's kidding," Gavin says. He starts up the porch, the wooden stairs creaking beneath his sneakers. The front door hangs open as kids come in and out, carry-ing cups of beer and laughing. We weave through them, making our way into a wide-open space that would probably be a dining room if it had any real furniture. Someone's set up a folding table, and a few people play flip cup by the light of the small electric lanterns scat-tered around the floor. Another group gathers around the keg in the corner, laughing as they fill sticky Solo cups with warm beer.

I look around for Riley, but she and her minions have vanished.

"Want a beer?" Gavin asks, nodding at the keg.

"Not yet," I say.

"Don't mind if I do," Deirdre says, heading for the keg line. Bass pounds through the floor, making it feel like the whole room is trembling.

"You have an eyelash," Gavin says. His features are in shadow, but I can still make out the strong lines of his jaw and nose. I hold my breath as he slides a hand over my cheek, his face so close that his nose is nearly touching mine. Gavin plucks the eyelash off my face and leans back.

"Your helpline sounds cool," he says, looking down at the eyelash pinched between his two fingers.

I open my mouth and then close it again. My mind is blank. "What?"

"The helpline you were telling me about? Is it something your school started?"

My mind catches back up with my mouth. I blink. "Oh, that. No. I started that."

Gavin nods. "Impressive."

"Thanks." I fall silent again. I can't think of a single thing to say to him, which is ridiculous. I've never felt so tongue-tied around a guy before. All I can think about is his face and smile and the way his skin felt when it brushed against mine. He could be a sculpture—all sharp angles and softly curling hair. A feeling rises inside of my chest—a hot, pounding *crush* feeling.

"You play?" Gavin asks, nodding at the folding table. Some girl flips a Solo cup on her first try, and a cheer erupts from the crowd.

"Flip cup?"

Gavin raises an eyebrow. "Unless you're scared."

"Scared?" I shove him playfully and he stumbles back a step, laughing. "For your information, I don't just play flip cup, I *dominate*."

"Strong words. You want to go next?"

"You're on."

We take our places at opposite sides of the folding table as the latest round ends in a roar of cheers and laughter. Someone hands us each a sticky cup, beer sloshing over the rim. Gavin catches my eye as we wait for the rest of our teams to take their places.

He winks. "Don't worry, I'll go easy on you."

I shake my head at him, a grin tugging at my lips. "You're going to get your ass kicked."

We raise our cups, clink, and start to drink. I finish first and set my cup on the edge of the table. I flip it perfectly on the first try—my team wins.

Gavin shakes his head as the rest of the team high-fives me. "You weren't kidding."

"To show there are no hard feelings, I'll get the next round," I say.

I turn and make my way over to the keg with our empty red cups. Hope is already crouched next to it, a Solo cup in one hand, her long black hair sticking to her forehead. She seems to be trying to work the spigot, but she drops her cup on the ground a second before she manages to coax a stream of beer out of the hose.

"Hope!" I call, but she doesn't turn around. I push my way past the flip-cup players as she bends over to pick her cup off the floor. The triangular cutout in the back of her jumpsuit shifts to the side.

Bruises blossom across her skin. They're massive, stretching to the edges of her mid-back like ugly purple and blue flowers. Some seem old and half-healed, already fading to yellow. Others look fresh, the blood still close to the surface of her skin.

My cup slips from my fingers. Horror roots me in place, making everything numb. The acid taste of nausea hits the back of my throat.

Hope clumsily adjusts her jumpsuit with one hand, standing.

"Hope!" I call after her, grabbing her arm before she can disappear back into the crowd.

"Hey," she slurs, already a little drunk. "If you're looking for Deirdre, I think she went out back."

"I'm not looking for Deirdre." I lean in closer, lowering my voice so the people around us won't overhear. "I saw your back."

Hope blinks at me, but the expression on her face doesn't change. "Yeah? So?" she says.

"Those bruises—" I start, but Hope tugs her arm out of my hand a little more forcefully than necessary and then heads back across the room.

"Hope!" I call after her. But she doesn't turn around. I swear under my breath and start scanning the crowd for Deirdre, but I spot Gavin first.

He's watching us from across the room. The humor has left his face, and his shoulders are stiff with tension. He doesn't look like the hot, laughing guy I've been flirting with all night. His mouth is set, and his eyes have narrowed to slits. I follow his gaze, turning just in time to see Hope disappear into the crowd.

CHAPTER SIX

"I have to find someone to test my bleaching technique on by *this* weekend," Deirdre says. "It's impossible."

"That sucks," I say, sticking a hunk of Swiss cheese into my mouth.

We're at the front counter of Liquid, where Deirdre's working and I'm unpeeling my third Babybel cheese of the evening. Needles buzz in the background, and the smell of blood and sweat fills the air. Every few minutes, someone screams or groans from the back.

It's been two days since the Battle of the Bands. Two days since the party where I saw Hope's mutilated back.

"You don't even like being a redhead," Deirdre points out, interrupting my thoughts. She's staring at my hair a little too intently.

I swallow my cheese. "That doesn't mean I want to let you play drunk stylist."

"I won't be drunk."

"I don't want you playing sober stylist, either."

Deirdre pouts. She's been balancing her night shift at Liquid with daytime classes at Lurlene's Cosmetology School since graduating, despite the fact that she's never shown much interest in her own hair, nails, or makeup. I'm not letting her anywhere near me with the bleach.

She leans over the counter and tugs on one of my braids. "I could just do a few strands—"

I swat her hand away. "No."

The phone rings and Deirdre groans, plucking it off its cradle. "Liquid Courage," she says into the receiver.

I turn around, leaning my back against the counter as she talks up whoever's on the phone. Pics of naked ladies adorn the walls around me. Half of them are torn from the pages of girly mags, and the other half are photos of pornographic tats on men's arms and shoulders and backs. Santos is a total perv.

Unfortunately, that didn't stop me from making out with him at their summer party a few months ago. I cringe at the memory. I need to learn to stop kissing gross guys.

My cell vibrates inside my pocket. I tug it out. There's a text from a number I haven't seen before.

Bible study tonight? There will be pizza . . .

Bible study means Gavin. I picture his blond curls and the freckles on his neck. Then the image disappears, replaced with the purple and yellow bruises blossoming across Hope's back. The way Gavin's eyes narrowed to slits as he watched his sister from across the room.

I close my eyes, squeezing the phone between my fingers. Those bruises could be from sports, or an accidental fall down the stairs, or a million other things.

My phone vibrates. Gavin again.

I'm not above bribing you. How does a root beer float sound?

I hesitate, thumb poised above the screen.

I type back, **I prefer my ice cream unfloated.**

"Who're you texting?" Deirdre asks, hanging up the Liquid Courage phone.

"Nobody," I say. My phone vibrates again.

Never mind. This could never work.

"That's a lot of texts for nobody." Deirdre grabs the phone from my hand before I can write back.

"Hey!" I lunge for it, but she's too quick.

"*Gavin?*" she says, squinting up at my screen. "The *pastor's son?*"

"The pastor's son *you* pushed me into," I remind her, snatching my phone out of her hands.

"I pushed you into him so he could help you find your mystery caller, not turn you into a Christian cult freak." Deirdre slumps in her chair behind the front desk. "Are you really thinking about going to Bible study?"

"Hope will be there," I point out.

Deirdre flicks a hunk of red wax across the counter at me. "You've got a problem, you know that?"

"You didn't see her bruises—"

"Bullshit. First you have to save this mystery caller, who was obviously just pranking you, FYI, and now you have to save Hope. You just want to play the hero."

I stare at a naked hula girl on the wall behind Deirdre's head, saying nothing. Deirdre considers me for a long moment, head tilted.

"Stop looking for someone to save," she says, finally. "Just go hang out with the hot guy."

I purse my lips. "He was *really* hot, wasn't he?"

"Yeah, but I bet he flirts with all the new girls. That's probably how they get people to join their cult."

I roll the cheese wax into a ball and throw it at her. She ducks and smirks.

My phone vibrates again. I look down at the screen.

I thought about it and I'm willing to give it a shot anyway.
We'll be like the Romeo and Juliet of ice cream.

"Cute," Deirdre says, reading the text over my shoulder. "Go for it. I'll pull you out if he turns you into a Stepford wife."

"Or worse, *Riley*," I mutter. Deirdre laughs.

I type I'm in into my phone and hit send.

Bible study is at Holy Grounds coffee shop, Gavin texts me as I'm heading over to Christ First on my bike. I read the name twice.

"The hell?" I mutter, sliding the phone back into my pocket. Braving the zombie teens to help someone was one thing. But now I'm going on a Bible study date at a Jesus-themed coffee shop.

Holy Grounds isn't so much a coffee shop as a tiny, shack-like building on the other side of the Christ First parking lot. The windows are small, dirty, and framed with tiny Christmas lights that somehow make the place look crummy instead of cheery. The siding is all peeling, rotten wood. The only part of the building that actually looks stable is the freshly built staircase leading to the front door.

I send Deirdre a text: If you don't hear from me in an hour, check the murder hut in the Christ First parking lot.

She writes back: If you die, can I bleach your hair?

Snickering, I lock up my bike and climb the stairs, pushing the door open, shrugging off the October chill in the night air.

"Whoa," I murmur, stepping inside. No murder shack vibe in here. Black-and-white tile stretches across the floor, and the walls are painted a cheery yellow. The place is almost cute. Vintage furniture sits in a circle at the back of the room, and I can hear people talking and laughing. The smells of pizza and coffee linger in the air.

I stop at the front counter. The barista wears a T-shirt that reads JESUS IS MY HOMEBOY.

"What can I get for you?" he asks.

"Um, you guys have cold brew?"

The barista nods and starts filling a plastic cup with ice. A Moses bobble-head doll sits next to the cash register. The sign attached to the coffee tin next to him reads LET MY PEOPLE TIP!

I flick his head, sending it bobbing up and down. "What's the deal with this place?"

"Holy Grounds?" The barista hands me my coffee and takes my five-dollar bill. "What do you mean?"

"Is it a coffee shop, or is it part of the church?"

"It's a coffee shop owned by the church. The youth group took a donation to buy it last spring and then spent the whole summer fixing it up."

"Why?"

"Pastor Joe wanted the community to have a place for teens to hang out with other believers and talk about religion and Jesus without judgment," the barista explains, handing me my change. "Christ First is all about fellowship."

I frown. *Christ First is all about fellowship.* Gavin said

almost the exact same thing at Battle of the Bands. It's like they're reading lines.

"Thanks," I say, shoving a dollar into the Moses tip tin. Pastor Joe can say he opened this place for the community, but it sounds to me like he opened it so "believers" didn't have to sully themselves by drinking coffee with the heathen hordes. Except for the Bible study group in the back, the place is empty.

I spot Gavin and Hope sitting on an old sofa with the rest of the group. Wooden stools and armchairs have been pulled into a loose circle around a coffee table piled high with pizza boxes. It looks like they've already started. Riley is talking.

"I know we're supposed to be leaders in Christ, but it's so hard trying to be a role model all the time," she's saying. The rest of the group sits in a circle around her, listening intently. "People look up to me. They expect me to live up to impossible standards. It's like I'm never allowed to mess up."

She pauses and wipes her nose with a napkin. I take a sip of coffee to keep myself from commenting. Am I really supposed to feel bad for *Riley*, queen of everything, when there are child soldiers in Uganda?

Gavin spots me and lifts a hand in my direction. Riley follows his gaze and shoots me a deadly look. She tries to hide it with a welcoming nod and a tight smile, but

I've known Riley for long enough to catch the way her nostrils flare.

I wiggle my fingers at her. If I'm already pissing Riley off, I must be doing something right.

Gavin stands and loops an arm around my shoulder, pulling me into the circle.

"Hey, guys," he says. "This is Brooklyn. I think some of you met her at Battle of the Bands Friday night."

The crowd smiles and helloes. I squeeze in next to Gavin, and Hope waves from his other side.

"It's *so* good to see you again," she says in that lilting way she has of talking.

Pastor Joe stands, clasping his hands together in front of his chest.

"Welcome, Brooklyn." He flashes me a wolfish smile. "And Riley, thank you for your confession. It shows a lot of strength to admit your weaknesses. That's what Jesus meant when he said that the meek shall inherit the earth."

Riley nods, the napkin balled up and forgotten in one hand. Pastor Joe pauses, the skin at the corners of his eyes crinkling as he lets the rest of us take in the message. The group around him nods in agreement.

Riley flashes him a teary smile. "You always make me feel strong."

Pastor Joe shakes his head. "I can't take credit. That's the man upstairs," he says, pointing at the coffee shop's low ceiling.

A few people laugh. I try not to roll my eyes. He talks about Jesus like he's just another bro. He's an adult man with an imaginary friend.

Pastor Joe continues talking about the meek and the kingdom of heaven and *blah blah blah*. I suck down another sip of iced coffee.

Gavin nudges me with his elbow. "I would have bought that for you."

I pull the straw out of my mouth. "You can reimburse me if you want."

Gavin's eyes get that cute squinty look to them. Like he's trying not to laugh. He leans closer. "You got change for a five?"

"Who'd like to go next?" Pastor Joe asks. The group looks around expectantly.

"Come on, someone must have something to confess," Pastor Joe says. "Laura, what about you?"

A tall girl with white-blond bobbed hair nods. She has an angular, arresting face and makeup that's so perfectly applied it looks Photoshopped.

"I guess I've been struggling with vanity lately," she admits, weaving her fingers together. "I spend too much time looking into the mirror, trying to get my makeup just right. I should focus on more important things . . ."

Hope catches me staring and leans across her brother's lap. "If they made an Instagram filter called Laura,

I'd be all over that shit," she says under her breath. "Isn't she perfect-looking?"

It's a little weird hearing the pastor's daughter say "shit" *during* youth group, but I look up at Laura, and Hope's totally right. Vanity pays off. Her red lipstick comes to a perfect cupid's bow, and it doesn't smudge when she takes a sip of coffee. Twin feathery light wings of black eyeliner swoop away from her eyes.

"I think you're being too hard on yourself, Laura," Pastor Joe says. Laura shakes her head.

"You don't understand," she says, gripping her coffee cup tighter. "I can't look away from the mirror until everything is perfect. I feel like something bad would happen to me if I did."

Pastor Joe reaches forward and squeezes Laura's hand. "Have you tried praying about this?"

Laura nods. "Yeah. But it isn't working. It doesn't feel like God's listening to me anymore."

"God is always listening," Pastor Joe says. "The rest of you, bow your heads. Let's pray."

Gavin grasps my hand while Pastor Joe reaches for the other. I'm not sure what to do, so I take it. I haven't held hands with anyone else since playgroup. Gavin's hand is warm and soft, but Pastor Joe has calluses on his fingers.

The rest of the group bows their heads.

"Heavenly Father," Pastor Joe says in a low, rumbling voice. Everyone falls instantly and completely silent. "We know that you ask a lot of us. That you *expect* a lot of us. But sacrifices are a part of faith. No man can experience the glory of the Father without first making himself low."

Pastor Joe holds my fingers too tightly.

"You sent your only son, Jesus Christ, to die on a cross for our sins. You saved our souls with that one act of love. Now it's our turn to live up to you. To be worthy of the great gift you've given us. From Matthew 5:29: *'If your right eye causes you to sin, gouge it out and throw it away. It is better for you to lose one part of your body than for your whole body to be thrown into hell.'"*

A few people murmur in agreement. I crack open my eyes. Were they even listening to what this freak just said?

"Lord, we need your help tonight. *Laura* needs your help. Help her find the strength to throw away the parts of herself that cause her to sin, so that she too may walk in the light. Be with Riley and Laura as they struggle against sin and strive to walk alongside you. Be with the rest of us as we try to live in your image."

I want this to be over. I want to pull my fingers out of this creepy old man's hand. But every other head is still bowed, every other eye clenched shut. I look at Gavin.

His and Hope's eyes are both closed. As they pray, Gavin weaves his fingers through Hope's, automatically. There's something different about her face now, when she doesn't think anyone can see her. She looks vulnerable. Scared. Gavin squeezes her hand, and a flicker of pure pain moves across her features, then vanishes.

"Amen," they recite together.

"Can I walk you home?" Gavin asks when the group finally starts to break up. We're standing outside the shop, next to my bike. I loop the chain over one shoulder, looking around for Hope. She's standing in the middle of a group of church girls, talking animatedly.

She's been surrounded by people all night. Like she doesn't want to be alone.

"Sure," I say, wheeling the bike between us. Gavin waves goodbye to Hope and the rest of his friends, and we walk away from the tiny coffee shop and down the twisting sidewalks back to my neighborhood. We don't talk, but the silence is nice. Like being with an old friend. Gavin bumps his shoulder against mine as we walk and then grins at me, shyly.

It's fully dark now, the only light coming from the dim streetlamps and the half-moon hanging in the sky above us. I stop at the sidewalk leading up to my front door, my house's twin Gothic towers casting a shadow over our heads.

Gavin leans his head back, his mouth dropping open. "*This* is where you live?"

"Creepy, right?"

"That's one word for it." Gavin points to the highest window. His gold hair and blue eyes look pale in the darkness. "I bet your dad is watching us from right there."

"My mom, actually. With a shotgun."

"Seriously?"

"Nah. She only brings her gun out when I'm on a date."

Gavin turns so that his whole body faces me. The moon hangs over us, casting the trees and sidewalk and dead grass in silver. He's not that much taller than I am. When he faces me straight on like this, our bodies line up perfectly—eye-to-eye, shoulder-to-shoulder, mouth-to-mouth. My heart stills. I wonder if he's going to kiss me.

Gavin tugs on one of my braids. "You're going to get me into trouble, Pippi."

I frown. "Pippi?"

"Pippi Longstocking? Look her up. You're like the hotter, hipster version."

I lean just a little closer, my hands pressed to his chest. "You think I'm hot?"

"I thought that was obvious." He rolls his lower lip between his teeth. "I should head home."

I feel a twinge of disappointment. No kiss?

"Text you tomorrow?" he adds.

I nod. "Yeah."

He walks down the sidewalk backward, like he wants to savor every second he has to look at me.

I watch him, too, but an image flashes into my head as I drink in his wicked smile and little-boy freckles—Gavin taking his sister's hand during the prayer circle. Squeezing her fingers. Like they were hiding something.

Deirdre's voice echoes in my head: *Stop looking for someone to save.*

Moonlight bounces off Gavin's hair, turning the blond to silver. Shadows hide his face. He's been the perfect gentleman since we met. He listened when I talked about the helpline, and he looked straight into my eyes when he told me that no one at Christ First would have made that call. He's a good guy. I have no reason to think he's hiding anything.

But the doubt lingers, even after he rounds the corner and disappears.

CHAPTER SEVEN

Deirdre is leaning against the bike rack outside school on Tuesday afternoon. When she sees me walking toward her, she holds up a DVD case.

"*Flowers of Flesh and Blood*," she says, waving it in front of me. "I had it overnighted. You haven't seen this one yet, right?"

I kneel next to my bike and start working the combination. *Flowers of Flesh and Blood* is the second *Guinea Pig* movie, a Japanese horror series designed to look like real snuff films. I've been trying to get Deirdre to watch it with me for months.

I pull the lock off my bike and loop it over my shoulder, standing. "You threw up in the middle of the last one, remember? You said I'd have to kidnap you and tie you up to get you to watch another one?"

"I just didn't like when they were pulling out that girl's fingernails," Deirdre says, shuddering. "Nasty. But it's cool, I'm ready to give it another shot. You in?"

I cock an eyebrow, wheeling my bike off the sidewalk and onto the dead, flattened grass surrounding the school. "What's the catch?"

Deirdre shrugs, all innocence. "No catch. I just figured that, while we were watching, you might let me bleach your—"

"Deirdre."

"Come on! I'm desperate. If I don't get a model I'm gonna get an incomplete."

"That's what the Internet is for. Can't you just pay someone fifty bucks?"

"Come on, B, *please?*" Deirdre sidesteps through the grass next to my bike, holding the snuff film in front of her face like a mask. "I don't have time to find someone online. And you'd look hot as a blonde."

"It doesn't matter, because I can't tonight. I have a . . . thing."

Deirdre raises an eyebrow, instantly suspicious. "What kind of thing?"

"Gavin has band practice," I explain. "I said I'd stop by."

Hope texted me about it during lunch. She said Gavin hasn't stopped talking about me since Bible study last night, and I should swing by to watch him in his natural habitat.

I think about how Gavin called me a hot Pippi Longstocking and absently touch one of my braids. I have to bite my lip to keep from grinning.

Deirdre stops walking. "You're going to go *watch* him? Like a *groupie?*"

"Yeah," I say. Deirdre gives me a *WTF?* look. "What? You used to watch Stevie's practice all the time."

"And you told me I was being pathetic and needed a hobby."

"Whatever. Stevie was gross." Stevie was ten years older than Deirdre, worked full time at Drugmart, and had two kids that he never saw because he "didn't want to be tied down." "This is different. I'm just hanging out with a hot guy, like you told me to. Don't overthink it."

"Whatever you say," she mutters.

I climb onto my bike and kick off, leaving Deirdre holding the faux snuff film. She'll probably hide it under her bed as soon as she gets home. "I'll text you tomorrow, okay?" I call over my shoulder.

"I'm not holding my breath," she shouts back.

Gavin's band practice starts at six. I don't bother showing up at Christ First until 6:42, and even then, Deirdre's comment is still ringing in my ears. *Groupie.* I shove the church door open a little too hard. I'm not a groupie.

It smells like incense inside. The cloying scent fills my nose and leaves me a little dizzy. I breathe through my mouth, blinking a few times to adjust my eyes to darkness.

"Hello?" I call. The carpeted floors keep my voice from echoing. "Gavin? Hope?"

No answer. I'm in a wide hallway lined on either side with closed doors. I try one—locked. There are windows in the walls, dark windows that look into empty classrooms. I press my face to the glass. Beanbag chairs slouch in the corners, and colorful Bible posters hang from the walls. This must be the children's section of the church.

Someone wrote *I love Jesus* across the bottom of a chalkboard. Someone else pressed a tiny hand onto the board next to it, leaving a fingerprint in the chalk dust. The fingers are doll-like. Fragile.

In Hope's text, she said the band practiced in a room off the main auditorium. I make my way down winding halls, feeling lost until I hear the faint sound of music rising from the silence. I turn one last corner. Light spills from a door at the end of the hall, and voices mingle with the steady beat of drums. *Finally.* I start walking faster. This place is a freaking maze.

I poke my head through the door, expecting to see the whole band rocking out. But it's just Gavin and Hope sitting on a loveseat at the far end of the room, their shoulders pressed together, heads bowed over a laptop balanced on their knees. Music blares from the tiny speakers.

"Brooklyn! You came!" Hope calls, spotting me. Gavin's head jerks up. He slaps the laptop shut, and the music goes silent.

"What are you doing here?" he snaps.

I look from Gavin to Hope, something unpleasant twisting my gut. I feel like I just saw something I shouldn't. "I thought—"

"Obviously she came to see how brilliant you are, dummy," Hope says, swatting Gavin's arm. "Don't be a jerk."

Gavin lifts his hand to swat her back, but then the corner of his mouth twitches, and he drops it into his lap again. I feel another twinge of weirdness. The snuggling on the couch, the play fighting. They're so *touchy*.

"Hope invited me, actually," I explain, stepping the rest of the way into the room. "I figured she'd tell you before I got here."

Gavin clears his throat. "She must've forgot."

"It was supposed to be a surprise," Hope adds, flashing a smile. Her voice reminds me of the way Riley sounds when she's manipulating people into doing her bidding. It's too high and sickly sweet. Deirdre calls it the sexy baby voice.

Hope stands, stretching her arms above her head and

arching her back like a cat. Gavin glances up at her and then shifts his eyes away. He drums his fingers against his laptop.

Blood rises in my cheeks, making the room feel suddenly warm. I feel like Hope is playing me. I study her, trying to figure out her game.

She drops her hands back to her sides and smiles, a genuine smile that's so unlike her father's fake ones they should have another word for it. I feel a flicker of doubt.

I clear my throat. "Where's the rest of the band?"

"They left early so we could work on some new stuff." Gavin stands, abruptly, and he doesn't look me in the eye as he walks over to his guitar stand. He shoots Hope a look that I can't interpret and picks up his guitar.

"Maybe I should go," I say.

"Don't be ridiculous," Hope replies, walking to the mic stand.

Gavin looks up, finally meeting my eye. "Yeah. You should stay."

I hesitate. They sound like they want me here, but I feel like a third wheel.

"You can tell me how bad I suck," Hope adds, pulling out the microphone.

"Sure," I mutter, plopping onto the couch.

Gavin strums his guitar. The chords start out slow and choppy, like he's unsure of what he's playing. I shift, uncomfortably, on the couch. Hope clicks a button on the computer, adding a drum and bass line.

"You say that I spoil your weekends . . ." Hope purrs into the mic. Her singing voice is deeper than her speaking voice. It's raspy and throaty and . . . sexy. Not the kind of voice you'd expect to be singing about Jesus.

I glance at Gavin, but he doesn't look at me. His fingers trail over the strings of his guitar, but he doesn't seem to be paying much attention to them. He can't take his eyes off Hope.

". . . I'm just trying to make things better for you . . ." Hope's mouth is so close to the microphone it looks like she's going to swallow it. She shifts her gaze toward Gavin. *"But you know who you need . . ."*

I scoot to the edge of the sofa, sliding my elbows onto my knees. *They're brother and sister,* I remind myself. *They're brother and sister, they're brother and sister . . .*

Bass pounds up through the floor, making the carpeting beneath my boots tremble. Hope licks her lips.

"You make me humble. You make me kneel . . ." Hope crinkles her nose at Gavin, like they're sharing an inside joke. He grins, shyly, and then looks down at the floor.

You make me kneel. The lyric echoes through my head.

I'm off the couch and out the door before I have to witness even one more coy glance or wrinkled nose. Fuck this. Either Hope is flirting with her brother on purpose, to freak me out, or she's one of those controlling sisters who doesn't think anyone's good enough for him and she wants to scare me away. Either way, this whole situation is seriously twisted.

Footsteps thud down the hall behind me. "Brooklyn! Wait."

Anger pounds through me, making my hands tremble. I spin around. "What the hell was that?"

The crinkle appears between Gavin's eyebrows. "What are you talking about?"

"Are you kidding? You practically screwed her with your eyes. Did you think I wouldn't notice?"

Gavin shakes his head. "She's my sister—"

"I know! That's what makes this whole thing so messed up."

"Brooklyn, listen. I *wrote* that song we were playing. I was watching Hope because it's the first time we ever performed it in front of anyone else." He shrugs. "I was too nervous to see your reaction. I thought you might think it was dumb."

I open my mouth and then close it again. This had not occurred to me. I replay the scene in the music room, looking for cracks in his story, but all I remember is the way he snapped the laptop shut so quickly when I walked in. How he anxiously took his spot behind his guitar.

I swallow, staring down at my combat boots. "So Hope . . ."

"You're not totally imagining things." Gavin runs a hand back through his hair, shifting his eyes to his feet. "She gets like this sometimes. She's not actually trying to be a bitch, but she likes to push people's buttons and see if they push back. It's her way of figuring out whether you're cool."

I frown. People who've been badly hurt before come up with bizarre coping mechanisms to keep it from happening again. The kind of manipulation Gavin's describing sounds like textbook victim behavior to me.

Stop looking for someone to save. But I can't help myself. "Is she—"

Gavin wraps his hands around my waist, pulling me closer. "I don't want to talk about my sister anymore."

I'm thinking of Hope's bruises, but now Gavin's face is just a few inches from mine, and his fingers are resting below the waistband of my jeans. He moves his thumb and it grazes the skin below my tank top.

"I thought I saw something at the party the other night," I mumble. But my mind is still on Gavin's thumb. On the spot where he's touching me.

Gavin dismisses my concern with a jerk of his chin. "Don't let Hope suck you into her drama." He lets his fingers drop from my waist to my hand. He squeezes. "I actually wanted to talk to you about something else."

"Yeah?"

"The thing is, I don't want to just randomly hang out with you. I want you to be, like, my girlfriend. Officially."

His words hit me like a slap. The kinds of guys I hang out with "don't do labels." They stick around till they ghost or get bored. The last time a boy actually *asked* me to be his girlfriend was Kris Vaughn, in second grade, and when I said okay, he hit me on the shoulder and ran away and never talked to me again.

I swallow. Part of me wants to pull my hand away from Gavin's, just to show him I'm not a girlfriend girl. But another part of me can't help but notice how right his skin feels against mine.

"So that would make you my . . . boyfriend?" I ask, testing out the word.

"That's the idea." He frowns. "You're totally freaked, aren't you?"

"No!" I say. But Gavin tilts his head and cocks an eyebrow and I can't help laughing. He pulls me closer, so that I'm pressed against him. "Maybe a little," I admit. "I've never had a boyfriend before. What does it even mean?"

"Mostly that I get to do this." Gavin presses his lips to mine. The kiss lasts only a moment, but it seems like longer. His lips are soft and warm. I wrap my arms around his neck and lean into his chest. Everything else feels fuzzy and far away.

"I could be into that," I whisper, after he pulls away.

"So what do you think?" he asks, leaning his forehead against mine. "Want to give it a shot?"

I frown, but his face is so close to mine that I don't think he notices. Girlfriends meet parents and come by for family dinners and get all dressed up for school dances. I've always been more of a "share a beer in your basement when your parents aren't home" kind of girl. Meet up at the park after curfew. Skip the school dance to fool around in the car.

But Gavin is different than the boys who are into that. He's actually a good guy. I bite my lip and then nod. "Okay. Let's do it."

Gavin lifts my hand to his lips and kisses the inside of my wrist. "I should make sure you get home safe, then. *Girlfriend.*"

I smile. But the word still sounds strange.

Gavin walks me all the way home and gives me a kiss on the cheek as he says goodbye. I watch him turn the corner just as Elijah comes out of my house.

"Who was that?" Elijah asks, following my gaze.

I don't quite know how to wrap my tongue around the phrase. "My . . . uh, boyfriend."

Surprise flashes across Elijah's face, but then he blinks and it's gone.

"Poor guy," he says, smirking. "Careful not to eat him alive." And with that, he hops onto his bike and pedals back toward campus, leaving me alone in the dark.

CHAPTER EIGHT

After school the next day, I text Deirdre to meet me at The Wilderness. It's our version of a smoker's corner. A million years ago someone dragged a few old sofas and lawn chairs into the trees, and now it's where kids go to drink and smoke, play music, and avoid class. It used to be the place Deirdre and I spent most of our free time, back when she was still in high school.

Now, it takes her five minutes to text me back, and then it's only one word: *Busy*.

I groan and shove my phone into my pocket, ducking into the trees. She must still be pissed at me for ditching her yesterday. I consider texting back to tell her that I'll let her bleach my damn hair. I'm that desperate to talk to someone about Gavin. My *boyfriend*. If I have to go blond to get Deirdre's opinion, well, so be it.

Red and orange leaves crisscross the autumn sky above me, blocking out the sun. My sneakers pad against the beaten dirt trail. An empty vodka bottle glistens from the bushes, and I step on something that turns out to be a used condom. Gross.

I make my way into the clearing and spot Charlie—younger brother to Ollie, who owns the tattoo shop. He's stretched across a couch with springs poking through the fabric, his messy hair sticking out from his head at all angles. He holds a book over his face, his sneakers propped against a faded, plaid cushion.

"Hey, Charlie boy," I call. Charlie peeks over the top of his book and nods at me, flashing a sideways grin that shows off the dimple in his cheek. "What's—"

"Brooklyn?"

I swivel my head around at the sound of my name. Riley ducks into The Wilderness, grimacing as a tree branch snags on her delicate pink sweater.

"Riley?" I blink, wondering if I accidentally inhaled some incredibly strong weed. But it's not a hallucination. Riley is actually standing in the woods in front of me. A pair of fuzzy dice with naked ladies on them hangs from a tree behind her head.

"I thought I saw you come this way," she mutters, poking at the loose thread in her sweater. "Oh, hey, Charlie."

Charlie gives her a short, confused wave, the book lying, forgotten, on his chest. "Hey," he says.

"Pretty weird to see you here," I say to her.

"Now you know how I felt seeing you at Christ First." There's a sneer in her voice, but it doesn't show on her lips. She flashes me a wide, plastic smile. "Anyway, I just heard the news that you and Gavin were a thing. Like, officially."

"What? How did you hear that?"

The corner of Riley's mouth twists. She was probably hoping I'd deny it. I bet that's the only reason she followed me here. "Laura texted me. Gavin's a hottie. You're so *lucky*."

"But how did—"

"I'm on my way to meet Laura and Hope for fro-yo. Since you're basically Christ First royalty now, I figured you might want to join."

I can't decide which phrase makes me want to puke more violently: *fro-yo* or *Christ First royalty*. I glance over my shoulder. Charlie appears to be reading again. But his book is upside down, and he seems to be trying hard not to laugh.

I try to hide the venom in my voice. "Nah, I'm cool here."

"That's probably for the best. Having you there might make Laura feel weird."

"Why would Laura feel weird?"

Riley shrugs, staring down at the car keys dangling from her fingers. The key chain is a vibrant purple and reads JUST BREATHE. "You know. Because of their *history*."

She mouths the word *history*, like it's too awkward to say out loud. It's such an obvious Riley trick. I know I shouldn't bite, that she's just creating drama where there isn't any. She collects secrets like other people collect dolls or baseball cards. Her favorite game was truth or dare when we were little, and even her dares were just another way to get people to tell the truth. *I dare you to kiss the boy you have a crush on. I dare you to face your deepest fear.*

But curiosity gets the better of me, and before I can stop myself, my lips pull into a smile just as wide and fake as Riley's. "On second thought, fro-yo sounds like fun."

"That's *so* great! The other girls are waiting in the car. I've got Barbara's Lexus for the day, isn't that amazing?"

Barbara is what Riley calls her mother. "A-*may*-zing," I echo, hollowly.

Riley loops her arm through mine, steering me back into the trees. "Come on, I'll give you a lift."

My muscles go stiff, but I don't pull away.

* * *

The cashier at the fro-yo place looks at me like I'm lost. Maybe it's my T-shirt, which is black and sleeveless and reads LIFE IS A GRAVE. DIG IT. A skull covered in silver glitter stares out from below the words.

"Do you have chocolate?" I ask. The flavors here all have cutesy names. *Teen Dream. High School Crush. Bubblegum Kiss.*

The cashier doesn't blink. The harsh overhead lights turn her skin yellow. Her wide, vacant eyes make her look like a zombie. "Mocha or double chocolate chunk?"

I ask for a swirl of both and head to the back, where Riley, Laura, and Hope are already squeezed into a booth. The seats and tables and walls are neon pink with white trim, and Taylor Swift plays on an endless loop.

Basically, this place is hell.

The only other person who looks half as bored as I feel is Hope. She stares down into her ice cream, her eyes glazed over. She's woven feathers and beads into her hair, and she's wearing a long, multicolored skirt that makes her look even more like a boho princess. A boho princess trapped inside a pink plastic jail cell.

I pull a chair up next to her at the end of the table. The floor's been freshly mopped, and the chair legs leave shiny marks in the soapy water.

Riley is studying a napkin with lines of numbers printed on it, her lips pursed in concentration.

"It says a scoop of strawberry shortcake has 212 calories, but I got a kid's scoop, not an adult scoop, so what's that? Like 140?"

No one answers. Riley tosses the napkin into the middle of the table, muttering under her breath about how this is the reason America is fat. I catch Hope's eye as she spoons caramel-colored fro-yo out of a tiny bowl. She shoves it into her mouth to keep from snickering.

Laura picks up the discarded napkin and starts tearing it into tiny pieces. "I thought Josh was going to meet us?"

"Where were *you* when I broke up with Josh?" Riley snaps, stirring the fro-yo in her tiny bowl. "I've decided I need an older man in my life. Preferably someone with a car."

I swear I can actually feel my brain liquefying inside of my head.

"Like a college boy?" Laura asks, pursing perfectly lined, cotton-candy-colored lips. Riley shrugs.

"If I can find someone qualified for the job." She scoops up a tiny spoonful of strawberry fro-yo and lifts it to her mouth. "Too bad we only have that lame private school nearby. I bet Mississippi State boys are hot."

"Magnolia boys aren't that bad," I mutter, absently. I think of what Elijah said as he left my house last night. That I eat boys alive.

Riley blinks. "Oh, right. I forgot that your dad, like, *works* there."

I grit my teeth together so tightly that my jaw starts to ache.

Laura slides her elbows onto the table and fixes me with her perfectly lined eyes. "So you're with Gavin now, right? Like, *together* together?"

"News travels fast at Mountaincrest," Hope adds, tilting her head apologetically. "Laura overheard me talking about it with Gavin over lunch."

Laura swirls her fro-yo with a plastic spoon, then lifts a dainty bite to her mouth. "How'd you do it?"

"Witchcraft," I say. Hope snorts, but Laura doesn't even crack a smile. "It was a joke, guys."

"Funny," Laura says, her lips curling. It's the way someone would smile if they'd only ever read about it in books. She rests the spoon against her bright pink lips. "It's just that Gavin is so picky about who he dates."

"What do you mean, *picky*?" I ask. Maybe it's all the Taylor Swift getting to me, but my voice comes out sharper than I mean for it to.

Laura lifts an eyebrow. "I didn't mean to make it weird," she says, after a moment. "I've had a crush on Gavin for *years*, and he's never been interested. But you show up and like two minutes later you're together. *Officially*."

"Laura—" Hope starts.

Laura shakes her head, her voice rising. "What? Am I not good enough for him? Not pretty enough? What does she have that I—"

"Lay off!" Hope snaps. "It's not Brooklyn's fault Gavin wasn't into you."

Laura flinches, like Hope's words physically hurt her. These girls are like snakes. What the hell have I gotten myself into?

"You need to calm the eff down." The anger drains from Hope's voice, leaving it lilting and songlike again. "Gavin isn't the only guy in Friend. Who cares if he's with Brooklyn now?"

Laura's shoulders slump, and she taps her spoon against her teeth. "You're right," she says, shaking her head. "I know you're right. God, I'm sorry, Brooklyn. I swear I'm not always such a spaz."

Riley is oddly quiet through all this, and the corner of her mouth twitches upward, like she's trying to keep from smiling. So *this* is what she meant by history. She's such a drama whore.

"It's fine," I say, catching Riley's eye. I smile, refusing to give her the satisfaction of playing this game. Her shoulders stiffen. She goes back to poking her fro-yo with her spoon.

"Let me squeeze out, Hope," Laura says, standing.

She presses a finger to the corner of her eye, stopping a tear before it can roll onto her cheek and ruin her contouring. "I need to go to the bathroom and fix my face."

Hope scoots aside so Laura can squeeze out of the booth past her. Laura puts one foot down on the freshly mopped floor at the same moment that a guy hurries past—knocking into her shoulder.

"Hey!" she calls, as the platform heel she's wearing slips out from beneath her. She lurches forward, grabbing for my chair, her fingertips missing by centimeters. Her knees smack into the floor, and her head snaps forward. She throws her hands out to protect her face— she's still holding her spoon.

There's a sudden, sick pop. Laura releases a sound that's half sob, half scream, and tries to push herself up to her knees. Blood appears around her head, forming a thick, red pool.

I leap out of my chair and drop to my knees. "Laura? Shit, what happened? Are you okay?"

Laura cries harder. She puts a hand on the floor to push herself up, but it slips in the blood, and she lurches forward again. I catch her by the shoulders before her face slams into the floor a second time.

"You shouldn't move her," Hope says. But Laura sits up on her own.

The spoon juts out of her socket, the broken plastic

wedged around her eye. The white is bloodshot, and blood drips from her lids and crusts in her lashes. Laura looks at us, and her eyelids flutter.

"I . . . I can't see," she says, her voice trembling. "I can't see anything."

CHAPTER NINE

"Dr. Stephens's office, how can I help you?"

"Hey," I say, recognizing Elijah's voice. "Is my dad around?"

"He's with a student. Everything cool?"

"Not exactly." I slump in a hard plastic chair in the hospital waiting room, trying to keep my voice steady. "Can you tell him I'm at the hospital?"

Elijah swears. "Are you okay? Do you need me to get your dad?"

"I'm fine—one of my friends got hurt. Can you just tell him where I am?"

"Of course." Elijah is quiet for a moment, but I can still hear him breathing on the other end of the line, so I know he hasn't hung up. "Do you want some company? Hospitals suck. I could leave your dad a note and drive over . . ."

I smile, halfheartedly, flattered by his offer. "No, that's okay. I'm not alone."

"All right. Let me know if you need anything."

I tell him I will and hang up the phone. Fluorescent lights buzz from the ceiling. The floors smell like antiseptic. Riley and Hope sit next to me, but we don't talk. Riley stares into space, twisting a strand of hair around one finger. Hope has her arms curled around her knees, the tips of her sneakers hanging off the edge of her plastic chair. She keeps touching her eye.

Someone deep inside the hospital starts to cry. The sound echoes through the halls.

"Can't believe . . . ," Hope whispers to herself. She's been saying this every few minutes, but she doesn't seem to expect a response.

I close my eyes, replaying the scene in my head. I should have told Laura the floor was wet. I should have taken the spoon out of her hand. I should never have agreed to date Gavin. I should have—

I force my eyes open again. It doesn't matter what I *should* have done. I didn't do anything. It's too late to change that.

People trickle into the hospital over the next half hour. Teenagers, mostly—I recognize some of them from Bible study. They wave or nod at us and then take a seat in the waiting room without a word.

"Are they all Laura's friends?" I ask, as another group of kids wander in through the front doors.

"Youth group," Riley says. "They're here to pray for her."

After about an hour, the hospital doors whoosh open, and Gavin rushes inside. His T-shirt is only half tucked in, and his hair is mussed. My chest twists. I texted him about Laura, but I didn't expect him to rush right over. He sees Riley, Hope, and me sitting at the far side of the waiting room and starts toward us.

"Hey," he says, sinking into an empty chair. He leans in to peck me on the cheek. "Are you guys okay?"

"Laura was the only one who got hurt," I say.

Gavin shrugs off his jacket. "Has anyone talked to the doctor yet? Is she going to be all right?"

"A nurse talked to us when they first brought her in. She said . . ." Riley's voice cracks. She closes her eyes and covers her mouth with her hand.

"Laura won't ever see out of that eye again," I finish for her.

Gavin collapses against the back of the plastic seat. "That's terrible."

I nod, not sure what else to say. I didn't know Laura that well, but I'll never forget her accident. I keep hearing the low pop of the spoon sliding into her eye socket. I shudder.

Gavin places his hand on my knee. "Are you okay?"

I stare down at his fingers. "I need some air," I say.

"I know someplace we can go."

Gavin takes my hand and leads me away from Hope's vacant eyes, and Riley's hollow voice, and the chemical smell of antiseptic. The waiting room doors open, and we step outside.

Trees dripping with dead leaves line the parking lot, hiding the hospital from the main street. Quaint brick walkways wind around low one-story buildings.

"There's a little park around here," Gavin explains, ducking down an alley between two buildings. Dumpsters line the narrow space, sending shadows over the cracked concrete.

I raise an eyebrow. "I think I preferred the waiting room."

"Trust me."

We pick our way past empty candy wrappers and soda cans. A crow leaps from the dumpster behind me, cawing.

Then, after about a hundred feet, the alley opens onto a lush, green space. A canopy of tree branches stretches overhead, blocking the sky. Everything is manicured, trim, and neat. Shrub-filled concrete planters dot the lawn, surrounding stone birdbaths filled with crystal-clear water.

"Whoa," I say, dropping onto a wooden bench. A marble cherub statue glows white in the moonlight. Tree branches send crooked, twitching shadows over his face, making it look like he's winking. "What is this place?"

"Technically it's part of the rehab hospital," Gavin explains, sliding onto the bench beside me. "I have this friend who was in a motorcycle accident earlier this year. His therapists had him walk around back here until he regained full mobility with his leg. It's technically off limits to the rest of the hospital."

"Does that mean no one else will come out here?"

"If we're lucky." Gavin drapes his arm over the back of the bench, his fingers grazing my shoulder. For the first time since we got to the hospital, I'm not thinking of the sound the spoon made as it slid into Laura's eye socket, or what I could have done differently.

I'm thinking of how Gavin's knee is resting against my knee. I'm thinking that we're alone in a beautiful, secluded park.

Gavin drops his hand onto my shoulder and squeezes. "I'm glad you're okay."

"I still can't believe that happened."

"God works in mysterious ways," Gavin murmurs. I press my lips together. In my opinion, Laura's accident was less about God and more about a wet floor and a poorly positioned spoon. But I don't want to spoil the mood.

I drop my head onto Gavin's shoulder and close my eyes. A cool breeze sweeps past me, lifting the hair from the back of my neck.

Gavin's lips press against mine. He slips his hand around my waist.

My mind goes blank the moment Gavin starts to kiss me. I press my hands against his chest, feeling the hard muscles beneath his T-shirt. He pulls me closer, his kisses hungrier. His tongue slips through my lips. His fingers fumble around at the bottom of my shirt, and then they're pressed against my skin. I shudder.

This is nothing like our shy, sweet first kiss outside of the music room last night.

"Is this okay?" Gavin asks, lips moving against my lips in a half kiss. Instead of nodding, I move my leg over his lap, straddling him. His body goes stiff, and I wonder if I went too far. But then he relaxes into me. His hands crawl up the back of my shirt, finding the bottom of my bra.

He hesitates. Then he unlatches my bra with a flick of his fingers.

I don't want this to stop. After all of the horror of the afternoon, I just want to feel good and young and happy. I dig my fingers through Gavin's hair and tighten my knees around his hips. He runs his hands over my bare back, his breathing coming fast and hot. I drop my hands to his waist, fingers fumbling for the button on his jeans.

"Wait—" He pulls away from me, panting. "We can't."

"Why?" I ask, gasping.

"We shouldn't. Not like this."

I lean back, still crouched on his lap. "Why not? This place is sort of perfect."

Gavin kisses me, lightly, on the lips. Then, holding me around the waist, he stands, lifting me off his lap and setting me back down on the bench. Alone.

I sigh and lean against the wooden slats. "Tell me you aren't one of those wait-till-marriage guys."

Gavin rubs a hand over his jaw. "I don't know. My dad thinks premarital sex is a sin, but I haven't made up my mind yet."

I lean toward him. "I can help with that."

Gavin doesn't take the bait. "It's only been a day. Let's get to know each other first."

I purse my lips. Every other guy I've been with has treated sex like a race. First one to the finish line wins. I kind of figured that was just how guys were, but taking it slow could be kind of hot.

I push myself to my feet, my bra straps still hanging loose beneath my skull T-shirt. "All right, Romeo. What do we do while we're waiting?"

Gavin pretends to think about this for a second and then offers me his hand. I roll my eyes.

"Hot," I say, dropping my hand into his.

But it *is* sort of hot. Gavin doesn't want to just fumble around with me in the dark. He wants to be with me. For real.

We hold hands as we walk out of the private park, back through the creepy alley, and over to the front entrance. The hospital doors open, releasing a cloud of air conditioning that coaxes goose bumps from my skin, making me shiver.

"Crap," I mutter, fumbling for my bra straps with my free hand. "Better make myself presentable."

Gavin hurriedly tucks in the corner of his shirt as we step into the waiting room. "Just make sure you—"

Pastor Joe is standing just inside the waiting room doors, and he turns at the sound of Gavin's voice. His eyes travel over Gavin's messy hair and untucked shirt. I drop my hand, leaving my bra unstrapped. My cheeks redden as he shifts his attention to me, his gaze lingering.

"Everyone's gone up to Laura's room," he says. "Why don't you join them?"

I glance at Gavin. He's looking at the floor, and there's a red tint to his cheeks. We start shuffling down the hall, but Pastor Joe drops his hand on my shoulder as I walk past.

"We must remember to keep our minds and bodies pure," he says, low enough that Gavin doesn't hear him. "Or else we'll let the devil in."

I swivel around to face him, my eyes narrowing. "What did you say?"

But Pastor Joe just pats my shoulder. "Laura's in room 308," he says. "I'll be up in a minute. Her parents are there now, and I told them I'd lead them all in prayer."

The door to Laura's room creaks open before I touch the knob. Riley's face appears.

"Oh, it's you," she says, pulling the door open wider. "Get in."

Gavin and I slip into the room. There are a dozen others crowded inside already. They've turned off all the lights and lined the windowsill with drippy white candles. Flames jump and tremble on the black wicks, making shadows leap across the walls. Everyone's face looks pale and hollow in the candlelight. Their eye sockets deep and dark. Their skin ghostly. A man in a police uniform hovers by the bed. I think he's there to take a statement, but then he reaches for the hand of the woman standing next to him—an older, plainer version of Laura—and I realize the cop must be Laura's father.

Laura lies on a thin cot in the center of the room, bloodstained bandages hiding her eyes. For a second, I think she's dead. Then she lifts a hand to her bandages, fingers twitching.

"Who's there?" she calls.

"It's just me," Gavin says, "and Brooklyn."

"Oh. Okay." Laura relaxes back into the pillows behind her, lowering her hand.

"Laura's nurse needs to replace her bandages, but Laura's afraid to take them off. We're going to form a prayer circle with Pastor Joe to offer her strength," Riley explains. She takes my hand in hers. "It's time to get started. Everyone form a circle."

The rest of the group shuffles forward, linking hands. Pastor Joe enters the room and joins the circle.

"Let us begin," the pastor says. "We have to humble ourselves before the Lord before we can ask for his mercy." Riley squeezes my hand. "Before we begin our prayer, let's go around the circle and unburden."

"Unburden?" I whisper to Gavin.

"Admit your sins," he whispers back. "Don't worry, you won't have to say much."

I resist the urge to roll my eyes. This is so weird.

"Wait," Laura says. She sits up, her mattress creaking beneath her. "I think . . . I think I'm ready."

"May the Lord give you strength," Riley says. She actually sounds sincere.

Laura unwinds the bandage with cautious, shaky fingers. The white cotton pools in her lap, blood blossoming across it like flowers. She lowers her head as she pulls the last of it from her face, her hair falling forward to hide her eye.

"Laura?" Riley asks, taking a step toward her. "Are you okay?"

Laura takes a deep breath. She looks up.

At first I think it's just the candles casting shadows across her face. But then she turns, and I realize it's not the light.

It's her eye. It's just . . . gone.

An empty socket glares out at us, deep and hollow. The tissue below has the tender look of raw meat. The skin around the socket has puffed to twice its usual size and swollen to a deep purple. An eyelid still clings to the ruined skin—blackened, like a flower petal about to fall off.

I cover my mouth with one hand so I don't scream.

Laura's remaining eye twitches around in its socket, looking from one horrified face to another.

A trickle of blood spills over her cheek, like a tear. "I'm not pretty anymore, am I?"

CHAPTER TEN

I'm in the school basement on Thursday night. Again. Staring at a phone that won't ring. Again.

This is the definition of insanity.

I dig my cell out of my pocket and pull up the Christ First mobile site. I couldn't stop thinking about Laura's accident and that empty, black eye socket the whole weekend. It's not just Laura, either. There was Hope's mutilated back, and the boy at the Battle of the Bands with his jaw wired shut. And Gavin mentioned that his friend was in a motorcycle accident.

There's a pattern here. It's like the Christ First kids are cursed.

My eyes glaze over as I scan dozens of photographs of smiling faces. I click on a link called "Prayer Circle," and a page loads, but it's just a long list of names and photos. A short paragraph at the top reads:

Through the blood of the lamb all will be healed. The following disciples have stumbled on their way to the kingdom of Heaven. Join Christ First in offering up prayers for their salvation and good health!

I glance at the list. Kevin, 17, broke his leg in a motorcycle accident. Derick, 14, broke his jaw after biting into an overcooked brownie. Amanda, 15, contracted Lyme disease on a hike in the woods. The list goes on.

I drum my fingers against the table. The basement smells rank, like a pipe burst and there's something vile leaking onto the floor. The door at the top of the stairs creaks open, then slams shut. I sit up straighter, suddenly alert. It's late. The school should be empty.

A stair groans. Then a voice calls, "Hello? Anyone there?"

I relax, slumping back against my seat again. "Down here, Elijah."

Footsteps thud against the staircase, and then Elijah bounds into the room, looking very much like someone who hasn't just spent the last hour in a musty basement, stewing in the scent of sewer. Strands of hair fall loose from his bun. The fold lines in his T-shirt tell me he probably just put it on.

He hovers at the bottom of the stairs. Then he lifts one hand and points at me.

"You're here," he says, voice slurring. He sways a little as he crosses the basement and then drops into the chair across from me. "I knew you'd be here."

I raise an eyebrow. "Are you drunk? It's not even eight."

"No. I had two beers." Elijah groans and lowers his head to the table. "It might have been more than two."

"It's a Thursday night. Don't you have to study or something?" I poke the top of his head with my Sharpie. "Why are you here?"

Without lifting his head, Elijah attempts to swat the marker away, misses, and then drops his hand again, giving up.

"This is a helpline," he says, his voice muffled by his folded arms. "I need help."

"Traditionally, one *calls* a helpline. We're not a walk-in service."

"Oh." Elijah lifts his head, resting his chin on his hands. He leans forward in his chair, digging the cell out of the back pocket of his jeans. "What's the number?"

I glance at the phone. No one else is calling. It's not like we're going to tie up the line. I grab my last flyer, crumple it into a ball, and toss it at Elijah's head. It bounces off his forehead and lands on the table in front of him.

"Ow," he mutters, flattening the flyer with one hand. He taps his thumb on the cell phone screen, and a second later, the helpline rings.

I lift the phone to my ear. "Teen Helpline, this is Brooklyn."

"Hiya, Brooklyn," Elijah says in a singsong voice. He's definitely had more than two beers. "Hey, you sound pretty hot. How old are you?"

I kick Elijah under the table. He snickers.

"You said you needed help," I remind him. "What's up?"

Elijah scrubs a hand over the stubble on his chin. He's not smiling anymore.

"Right," he says. "The thing is, I'm not that great at talking about my feelings."

"The helpline's anonymous. You can tell me anything."

Elijah stands up, his chair legs scraping against the concrete floor. He turns so that his back is to me. "I broke up with Sloan today," he says, after a long pause. "We've been together since high school. I guess I'm feeling kind of weird about it."

I chew on the inside of my cheek. Elijah once told me that he and Sloan met their freshman year of high school. I figured they'd be one of those couples who were together their whole lives, telling fat grandbabies that they met when they were only fourteen.

"Why did you break up?" I ask.

Elijah is still facing away from me. He shrugs, his shoulders jerking up and down beneath his T-shirt.

"You can't see a shrug over the phone," I tell him.

"Right. Um . . . I don't know. I guess I was starting to get the feeling we were only together because it was easy. Like maybe we were both scared to be on our own."

"You're not scared anymore?"

"I am . . . but now I'm more scared of staying with someone I don't love."

He swallows, and I hear the sound echo into the receiver. The phone suddenly feels clumsy in my hands. When I first started this helpline, I expected people to call in about addiction and abuse and teen pregnancy. I gathered pamphlets and memorized phone numbers. There are no pamphlets for breaking up with your long-term girlfriend. I don't know what to say.

"I think you did the right thing," I say, finally. "You shouldn't be with someone you don't love."

"Yeah. Like you and that guy from the other day, right?"

"Gavin?" Gavin and I have not gotten to the "love" point yet, but I nod. "Yeah, sure."

Elijah takes the phone away from his ear and hits the end call button. I hang up my phone, too. I feel awkward without it pressed to my ear. Elijah and I have always been strictly acquaintances. We don't hang. We don't talk about anything more important than fruit protests. It's strange for him to unload on me.

As if reading my mind, Elijah turns back around. "My friends are all Sloan's friends," he explains. "They kind of hate me right now. I just figured you'd be good to talk to."

"Are you okay?"

Elijah shrugs. "Sort of. I'm sad and everything, but I think it was the right thing to do. I've known for a while that we were just treading water."

He sits down again.

"You're pretty great at this," he says, tapping a knuckle against the table. "Talking to people. Listening."

"Too bad nobody ever calls."

"What about that girl you were telling us about the other day? The one who said someone was hurting her?"

I weave my fingers together, staring down at my clenched hands. "Couldn't find her."

"That sucks." Elijah picks a soda bottle cap off the floor and spins it on the table. "I bet you could have helped."

"Deirdre thinks it was a prank," I say, watching the bottle cap spin. It barely makes half a rotation before he has to pick it up and spin it again. For a long time the only sound in the basement is plastic sliding over wood.

"Did you have a crush on me when we first me?" he asks, out of nowhere.

"No," I say. Too quickly, probably. Elijah started working for my dad last year, when I was a sophomore. He was cute, and he was always reading some indie comic book with rad art on the cover, and he listened to bands I'd never heard of.

Elijah twirls the bottle cap again. "Oh. I thought maybe you did."

My face feels a little hot—thank God I don't blush. "Why?"

He jerks a shoulder up and down. The movement makes him lose control of the bottle cap, and it shoots across the table. I slap my hand over it to keep it from flying to the floor.

"No reason," he says. He leans back in his chair, tapping both hands against the table, bongo drum style. "I should probably go. You've still got your . . ." He jerks his chin at the telephone sitting between us.

"Yeah," I say. I feel like he wants me to say something else. He screws up his face—lips pursed, eyes narrowed. Like he's waiting for something.

"Some guys I know are having a party tonight, if you want to stop by," he says. Then, before I can say a word, he stands in one quick motion and turns around. His shoes thud up the stairs.

"Text me the address?" I shout after him.

"Sure. See you later." The door opens and closes, and I'm alone again.

I stare at the far wall for a long moment, frowning. That was weird. Did he really come all the way over here just to tell me he broke up with Sloan? How drunk *was* he?

After a few minutes, it occurs to me that maybe he was hoping I'd ask him the same question he asked me, about whether he had a crush on me when we first met.

I pick up the bottle cap he was spinning and balance it on one finger. If he had a crush on me then, maybe he still has a crush on me now. Maybe that's why he broke up with Sloan. Why he came here.

My chest twists. I'm with Gavin, so this shouldn't matter. I touch my phone screen, and the list of prayer requests pops up. Motorcycle accident. Lyme disease. Broken jaw. Deirdre's voice echoes through my head:

You just want to play the hero . . . Stop looking for someone to save.

I stare at the phone screen until it goes dark. Maybe she's right. Maybe I should go to a party. But D's not talking to me right now, and it's not like I'm Miss Popular. She's one of the few people in this town that I can stand.

I click over to my text messages. I bet Hope likes parties. And I'd feel better about hitting up Elijah's party if my boyfriend's sister is with me.

What the hell? I shoot her a text: **What are you up to tonight?**

CHAPTER ELEVEN

The sidewalks near Magnolia State crawl with laughing college students, all stumbling toward a brightly lit house at the corner. I glance up as we drive past, recognizing the Greek letters affixed to the brick.

Hope inches her car up to the curb. "You didn't tell me this was a frat party," she says, killing the engine. She pulls a floppy leather purse onto her lap and digs out a tube of lipstick.

"I didn't know Magnolia State had fraternities." Or that Elijah would be caught dead at one.

Hope flips the visor and studies her reflection in the mirror. "I've dated my share of freaky hipster boys. Trust me. They like to party and watch girls get wasted, too," she says, sliding lipstick over her mouth. It's such a dark purple it almost looks black. She smacks her lips together. "How do I look?"

I study her, a little jealous of her fierce makeup and confident smile. "Didn't realize you were such a party girl."

"We're only young once, right?" Hope drops the lipstick back into her purse and zips it shut.

"It doesn't bother your dad?"

Hope shrugs. "If he knew about it, maybe."

"So he'd be totally pissed if he knew you were out with me right now."

"Whatever. He gets mad when I wear tank tops and watch R-rated movies. There's no pleasing that man. You said your dad teaches college, right?"

I nod. "Yeah."

"Lucky. I can't wait to go to college." Hope pushes her car door open and climbs out. I follow her.

Bad music pours from the windows of the frat house, and a stream of college girls wearing next to no clothing head up the stairs to the front door. I slip my jacket off and toss it back into the car. I'm wearing a cropped tank underneath, and there's a strip of bare skin between the top of my jeans and the bottom of my shirt. Hope slips her arm through mine and tugs me toward the party.

The house is packed. We have to push against the bodies in front of us just to get up the steps. Inside, they're all wearing masks—everything from rhinestone-and-feather-encrusted cardboard that just covers their eyes to full-on rubber monster heads. An early Halloween party. *Thanks for the heads-up, Elijah,* I think, picturing the sequin-covered skull mask I had saved from last year. It would have been nice to know we were supposed to dress up.

All the lights inside the house are off, and there's newspaper taped over the windows to shield us from the glow of the streetlights. Something bright flashes from a corner—a strobe light, I think. As it flicks on and off, I get glimpses of glazed eyes and twisted smiles beneath the rubber and cardboard masks.

"Fresh meat!" comes a voice from just next to my ear. I smell sour breath and wrinkle my nose, ducking away instinctively. A tall boy in a football jersey and gorilla face leans forward, his voice muffled by the rubber.

"You're new," he says, shoving a red Solo cup at my face. Sticky blue liquid sloshes over the side. "New girls drink free."

I don't usually take drinks from strange guys in gorilla costumes, but hey, it's a party. Elijah wouldn't have invited me if the guys here were dirtbags. I look around for him, but it's too dark to see much.

"Thanks." I grab the cup and hand it to Hope. "Drink this."

She wrinkles her nose. "What is it?"

I shrug, taking another cup from gorilla guy. He whoops and lifts his hand to high-five me, but I turn my back on him and push Hope deeper into the crowd.

"We'll see. Bottoms up!" I toss the drink back. It tastes exactly like melted Jolly Ranchers.

Hope lowers her cup and releases a tiny burp.

"Gross!" I wave my hand in front of my nose, laughing. "Did you really just burp?"

"I couldn't help it! It's all that blue raspberry crap." She wrinkles her nose and takes another sip. "It's starting to taste better, though."

"Really?"

She nods. Her lips are already a little blue. She'll be wasted before that cup is empty.

I drink some more blue raspberry garbage. "It was cool that so many people came out to support Laura."

"Sure! Christ First is good at shit like that."

I frown. "What do you mean?"

"They're all about praying and holding hands." Hope empties the rest of her drink. "When it comes to real problems, they're not interested."

The prayer requests flash in my head. "What real problems?" I shout over the music.

Someone bumps into my arm, knocking half my drink onto my chest. I swear, but the music swallows my voice.

Hope frowns. "What?" she asks, lifting a hand to her ear.

"Never mind," I say. This is a party, not a recon mission. It's too loud for a real conversation, anyway. Somehow, even more people have managed to shove their way inside. Their voices overlap, and I don't think I could follow a single conversation even if I closed my eyes and focused all of my attention on trying to pick one voice out of the hundreds.

Hope grabs my hand. "Let's dance!" she calls, dragging me over to a group of kids bouncing around in the middle of the room. She floats her hands over her head, closing her eyes and swaying her hips in time with the music.

Dancing could be good. I start bouncing along to the music, wiggling my hips and bobbing my head. After only a few minutes, I'm feeling unsteady. I look down at my drink, frowning. What the hell is in these things? I take another sip, then make a face and spit it back into my cup. No way am I finishing *that*.

Some guy wearing a Betty Boop mask grabs Hope by the hips, pulling her toward him. Betty's eyes have been hollowed out, and the mask hangs far enough off his face that I can't see his eyes. The darkened eyeholes remind me of Laura. I picture her empty eye socket and fluttering, half-ruined eyelid. I shudder.

Hope smiles and pushes him away as politely as possible, but a second later, he has his hands around her hips again.

"Hey!" I shout, wedging myself between them. "She said no."

A girl bumps into me, and I stumble into him. Suddenly everything seems too loud, too close. I'm already sticky with sweat and booze.

Betty reaches for Hope again, his hand grazing her back. Pain flashes across her face. She jerks away from him.

"I . . . I need some air," Hope murmurs, grabbing my arm. I shove my drink at Betty—"accidentally" spilling some blue crap over his ragged Betty Boop dress—and lead Hope back through the crowded main room, out the door, and onto the porch.

The cold hits me like a slap. It was so hot wedged between all those sticky bodies that I'd forgotten it's October and chilly enough after the sun goes down to make my teeth chatter.

Hope stumbles forward a few feet, pausing when she reaches the steps. I sit on the top step, and she slides down next to me, one hand clutching the bannister to keep her balance. "Thanks. I needed to get out of there."

"You okay?"

"I'm fine. That guy just kept touching me." Hope shudders and wraps her arms around her chest. She looks completely different than she did when we entered the party. The lipstick has all worn off her unsmiling mouth, and her eyeliner is smudged. She looks small and fragile. Someone easily broken.

A car alarm blares into the night, the whooping siren competing with the heavy bass still echoing from the party behind us. Hope wipes a tear from her cheek when she thinks I'm not looking.

"You want to talk about it?" I ask.

"Talk about what?" Hope tries for casual, but her voice is too high.

I drop my hand on her shoulder and give her a squeeze. "You seem down. Is it a guy?"

Hope releases a short, humorless laugh. "Trust me, you don't want to hear my sob story."

The car alarm stops blaring, and now the only sound is the rap music drifting from the party behind us. There's no moon tonight. Dim light pours down from streetlamps and flickers from living room windows. It's dark on the porch. I can barely see Hope's face.

"Does it have something to do with the bruises on your back?" I ask, carefully.

Hope jerks around to face me, her lips parted in shock. Even in the darkness, I can see that the color has drained from her face. "Did Gavin tell you?"

I blurt, "Tell me what?"

Hope looks at her knees. "You know. About . . ."

She doesn't finish her sentence. A buzzing sound starts in the back of my head. "Hope?"

Hope looks up again, staring at my face. "I'm adopted, you know. It's not like Gavin and I are really related."

The buzzing gets louder. I think of Hope resting her hand on Gavin's shoulder. Hope's knees leaning against his as they snuggled together on the couch.

"Yeah," I say, slowly. Hope shifts her red-rimmed eyes to the street and then back over to me. She's drunker than I realized. Her eyes don't stay focused.

"Don't be mad," she says, her voice hoarse. "He didn't even know you then."

"What happened?" I ask. I'm surprised by how calm I sound.

"We were in South America, on a mission trip with our dad. He'd gone over to the next village to meet this priest that everyone was talking about, and he was out late. Gavin and I were home alone, and these local kids had given him this bottle of rum. I'd never had rum before." Hope smiles, sadly. "I drank too much. Both of us did. It never should have happened, but we were so drunk, and it was warm outside, and there was a full moon." Hope swallows, squeezing her eyes shut. "I kissed him—just once, to see how it felt. But then he kissed me back and . . . We tried to stop, but . . ."

I lift my hand, stopping her. I can't hear any more of this. Adrenaline pumps through my chest, leaving my blood hot and my muscles tight. My body is all gasoline and lit matches. I feel like I could punch straight through a wall or lift a car over my head.

He's hurting me, I think, and something thick and sour hits the back of my throat. "Hope, did Gavin—"

"He didn't give me the bruises, if that's what you're thinking," Hope says. "He'd never hurt me. He thought he was in love with me after that night, but then our dad found out what happened and he . . ."

Understanding washes over me. "Pastor Joe is punishing you."

Hope's eyes flick up, meeting mine for a fraction of a second before moving to her lap again. "He says I . . . seduced Gavin. That I have evil inside of me. He's trying to help me."

I take Hope by the shoulders, forcing her to look at me. "Does Gavin know about this?"

Hope is quiet for a long moment. She finally nods, moving her chin only a fraction of an inch. "Gavin didn't believe it at first, but now he thinks our dad is right. What we did in South America was really wrong. He says I need to be made pure in the eyes of God."

A single tear crawls down Hope's cheek, reflecting the light from a distant street lamp. She brushes it away angrily, like it's betrayed her. I should comfort her. I should give her a hug and tell her it's all going to be okay. But I feel frozen.

Gavin *knew*. He knew that his father was beating his sister, and he did nothing. He told Hope she *deserved* it.

I lift a trembling finger to my lips. I kissed him. I let that slut-shaming asshole *touch* me. What Gavin said about his sister flashes into my head:

She can be kind of controlling . . . she likes to push people's buttons.

I stand so quickly that I nearly lose my balance. Even then he was trying to poison me against her, so I wouldn't believe her cries for help. The taste of blue raspberry rises in my throat. I think I'm going to be sick.

"We need to call the cops," I say. "You need to get out of that house."

"No police. You can't tell anyone about this." Hope grabs the bannister and pulls herself back up to her feet. "I thought the whole point of your helpline was that I get to stay anonymous."

I shouldn't be surprised to hear this after everything Hope just admitted, but I still feel like I've had the wind knocked out of me. "Of course. You're the one who called."

"Look, I'm not some fucking victim, okay?" Hope crosses her arms over her chest, squaring her jaw. "I only called because I wanted to talk to someone. I didn't think you'd show up at my church the next day."

"Hope—"

"I know that what they're doing is wrong, but there's nothing I can do about it. The people at Christ First love my dad. You saw Laura's dad at the hospital, right? He's the chief of police. I know because we've had him over for dinner twice. No one's gonna believe me."

I stare at Hope's face. She must've bitten her lip when we were dancing, because there's a tiny cut at her mouth, a bit of dried blood mingling with her purple lipstick. Other than that, she looks amazing. Her hair is tangled like a rock star, and the sweat on her face makes her skin glow.

She doesn't look like a victim. Gavin doesn't look like a predator. But that's the thing they don't tell you in the movies—nobody ever looks like who they really are.

I'm going to nail him to the wall for what he and his father are doing to Hope.

I'm going to burn them to the ground.

CHAPTER TWELVE

I load Hope into the passenger seat of her car, and she immediately rests her head against the window, eyes flickering closed.

"I'm just going to tell Elijah we're taking off," I say.

"Mmhmm," she murmurs. Her lips part, and her breathing grows a little deeper.

"Hope?" I snap my fingers in front of her face, but she doesn't move. A second later, she starts snoring lightly.

I nudge the car door closed with my hip. Hope doesn't stir.

I shove my way through sweaty bodies, waving off more offers of sticky Solo cups filled with blue liquid.

I ask a few people if they know where Elijah is, but no one's seen him. Some guy dressed as a robot tells me to try the second floor, third door on the right. I take the steps two at a time, anxious to get away from the drunken throng, but lose my nerve as soon as I'm standing in front of the door. He could be in there with a girl.

Elijah pulls the door open before I get a chance to knock. "Hey! I was looking for you."

"Yeah, sorry. I was with a friend, and things got kind of messy." Understatement of the century. "Are you alone?"

Elijah steps aside, pulling the door open wider. The room is tiny. A mini fridge sits under the window, and cheap furniture fills the rest of the space—twin-size bed, milk-crate bookshelves, a desk covered in band stickers.

"Is this your room?" I ask, stepping inside. Elijah shakes his head.

"Nah. I live in Howard Hall, but Sloan's on the next floor, and, well . . ." He scrubs a hand back through his hair, shrugging. "This is my buddy Alex's room. He's out of town for a few days and said I could borrow his bed."

"That's cool." I examine the space with new eyes, looking for signs of who Elijah is when he's not hanging around my dad. He's neat. There's no trash or dirty laundry on the floor, and sheets and blankets have been hastily pulled over the mattresses.

"You want a soda?" Elijah asks.

I shake my head and perch at the edge of his bed. Elijah digs around inside the mini fridge, grabbing himself a Coke.

"Why aren't you down at the party?" I ask. Bass thuds through the floor below me, making my boots tremble.

"Not really my scene." Elijah cracks his Coke and takes a drink. "I tried for a while, but it was starting to give me a headache." He frowns. "Is that why you stopped by? To drag me back down?"

He looks a little hopeful. I almost feel bad that I have to leave. "No, actually, there's something I need to go deal with."

"Is everything cool?" Instead of sitting next to me, Elijah grabs the chair from his desk and drags it over. He leans forward, propping his elbows on his knees. "You look kind of upset."

I swallow. Hope's story echoes inside of my head, like a song on repeat. I can't think about it for more than a few seconds without hot anger filling my gut.

"I figured out who the helpline's mystery caller is," I explain. And then I blurt out the whole story, from the first time I spotted Hope's bruises, to getting involved with her brother, to Hope's confession about what happened in South America. "She's downstairs sleeping in the car right now, but I can't exactly take her home, and I can't tell my parents what's going on. You saw how they reacted when all I did was ride my bike to a freaking church. But I can't just do nothing."

"You'd be surprised by how many people do nothing," Elijah says. "It's a lot easier to close your eyes than admit what's going on."

I drop my head into my hands, frustration building in my chest. "No one at Christ First is going to believe me. They practically worship Pastor Joe."

Elijah stands, his chair creaking. He drops onto the bed next to me. "It's not easy to do the right thing," he says.

"It's impossible," I mutter, not bothering to lift my head.

Elijah is quiet for a long moment. He clears his throat. "My dad died a couple of years ago, and I'm kind of not talking to my mom."

I lift my head, resting my chin on my hands. "What?"

Elijah stares at his hands. He weaves his fingers together and then pulls them apart.

"It's a long story," he says, after a moment. "My dad wasn't a great guy. He . . . let's just say that he and Pastor Joe had similar ideas about how to punish their children."

"Elijah . . . ," I say, sitting up straight.

Elijah shakes his head. "It's okay. I mean, *now* it's okay. But back when he was alive, I didn't know what to do. My mom got the worst of it, but she wouldn't leave

him. I was too young to help her. I kept thinking someone would step in and do something. That a teacher or
my baseball coach or *someone* would see the bruises and
try to help. But no one ever did."

"What happened?"

"Act of God." Elijah shakes his head, like he can't
believe he's saying this out loud. "I never thought there
was a God. My mom and I weren't religious or anything
like that. I didn't pray. But I don't know how else to
describe what happened. My dad didn't drink, but he
stopped at a bar to have a beer with some guys from
work, and he must've had too many because he crashed
his car on the way home. He drove right into a tree and
slammed his head into the steering wheel."

"That's what killed him?"

Elijah nods. "It was weird—there weren't any other
cars on the road, so the police think he must've swerved
to keep from hitting a deer. I was only thirteen when
it happened, and it felt . . . it felt like God answered a
prayer I never spoke out loud. It sounds horrible, but
that was the best day of my life."

I'm not sure what to say, so I stare at a hole in my
jeans. A bit of my skin shows through, all pink and fragile. The lightest touch could tear it open. I swallow and
cover the hole with my hand. It hurts to think that there
are people in the world who treat bodies so horribly.

"It's actually why I wanted to study religion with your dad. To see if I could find a real answer to what happened." Elijah is silent, then nudges my leg with his. "Are you okay in there?"

Without thinking, I drop my hand onto his knee and squeeze. Elijah puts his hand on mine. It covers my fingers entirely. His palm is warm.

"I'm so sorry you had to go through that," I say.

"Me too." Elijah's voice is deeper than it was a moment ago. It sends goose bumps up my arms. "I think that what you're doing for Hope is really brave. Nobody did that for me."

I lift my head, meeting his eyes. "I would have."

"My guardian angel," he murmurs, smiling.

I squeeze his hand. "People have to look out for each other."

Elijah shifts closer to me, his leg pressing into mine. I can feel the heat of his body through his jeans.

"So this guy you were dating. The brother. Is that still a thing?" he asks. His voice is deeper.

"It's over," I say, my voice firm. It was over the second Hope told me what happened to her. "I'm telling him tonight."

I look up. Elijah's nose is just inches away from mine. He leans closer, his lips parting.

I close my eyes a second before he kisses me.

CHAPTER THIRTEEN

I can still feel the weight of Elijah's lips against mine as I head back to Hope's car a few minutes later. The memory sends shivers racing through me. Part of me wishes I could run right back up to his room and forget about Hope and Gavin and Pastor Joe. But Hope's waiting for me.

It's cold. I forgot my jacket in the car. Goose bumps travel up my arms and legs. Wind passes through the trees, making the branches shiver. Dead leaves fall to the sidewalk. I climb into the driver's seat of Hope's car, slamming the door behind me. Hope stirs.

She groans, her eyelids flickering open. "Where'd you go?"

"Just told Elijah we're taking off. Give me your keys."
I hold out my hand. I only had a few sips of that blue
crap, and everything that's happened over the last hour
has sobered me up. "And I don't know where you live."

"By the church," Hope mumbles, fishing a key ring
out of her purse. "The yellow house with the blue door."

I nod and fit the key into the ignition, starting the
engine. Hope leans her head back against the window.
A second later, she's snoring again.

I drive down the winding streets of Friend, back
toward Christ First. There're no cars on the road, but
jack-o'-lanterns stare out from porches and windows and
front yards. The candlelight makes their eyes glimmer,
their smiles dance. They look like they're laughing.

I find Hope's house easily. It's right across the street
from Christ First, the blue door clearly visible, even in
the darkness. A tire swing hangs from the tree out front,
and there's a picnic table next to the patio, a dried-up
plant in a clay pot perched in the middle. It's the kind of
place where you would have played cards, eating cookies
and drinking lemonade, while citronella candles kept the
mosquitos at bay.

I glance at Hope. She's fast asleep, her face pressed up
against the window, hair plastered to the back of her neck.

"Home sweet home," I say. When Hope doesn't move,
I push the car door open and climb out. She groans and
shifts in her seat as I pull her door open.

"*Wherearewe?*" she mumbles, stumbling out of the car. I hadn't realized she was so out of it.

"Your place." I take her by the elbow to steady her. It's late, and the darkened windows of Hope's house show no signs of life inside. No shadows, no light creeping through the slats in the shutters. Gavin and Pastor Joe are probably asleep. Hopefully they'll stay that way.

Dry grass crunches beneath our feet. I help Hope across the yard and up the stairs to the porch. A wooden step creaks beneath us, and I go still, heart hammering.

"What are you doing?" Hope says, giggling.

I hold a finger to my lips. "I don't want to wake your dad."

She nods and mimes zipping her lips shut. "We should take the back door, then. It doesn't creak."

Quietly, I help Hope down the stairs and around to the back of the house. An old metal swing set sits in the yard. The chains creak as the swings sway in the light breeze.

I find the back door and fit Hope's key into the lock—it opens with a soft click. I pull the door open. The hinges don't creak.

"See?" Hope says in a too-loud whisper.

I nod. "Clearly you've snuck home after curfew before. Can you make it to your room from here?"

Hope nods and places one platform-clad foot inside. She missteps, and her ankle twists, causing her to lurch forward. I grab her around the waist before she hits the floor.

"Easy," I say. I pull the back door closed behind us, holding the knob until it's firmly settled in place so the lock doesn't click. "Why don't we take those off?"

Hope looks down at her shoes like she didn't remember she was wearing them. I help her take them off and then slip my boots off, too, leaving them by the back door. My socks muffle the sound of my footsteps.

"Where are we?" I dig my cell phone out of my pocket and switch on the flashlight. A white beam appears, illuminating a small, musty basement. There isn't much down here. An old washer and dryer sit beside the far wall, a basket of dirty clothes on the floor in front of it.

"Stairs are over there," Hope mumbles. I move my phone, and the light hits a narrow staircase in the far corner of the room. Hope's not making it up those stairs on her own.

"Come on," I say, taking her by the arm. The concrete floor is freezing, and the cold creeps up through my socks, chilling the bottoms of my feet. But at least I don't hear movement upstairs.

Every creak of the wooden stairs seems to echo. Every beat of my heart seems to boom. I press my lips together, trying to hold my breath, but each inhale sounds raspy and loud. Hope can barely put one foot in front of the other. I have to put my cell phone away and practically carry her up the stairs.

Be cool, I tell myself. I blink again and again, trying to get my eyes to adjust to the darkness. It's like trying to stare through oil. I can't see anything. I reach the top of the staircase and lower my hand to the doorknob, slowly twisting the brass handle.

It takes a moment for my eyes to adjust to the light. We're in a small kitchen. The fridge hums, quietly, next to me, and water drips from the faucet. I step forward, my socks slipping on the linoleum.

"Where's your room?" I ask. Hope mumbles something and pulls away from me, disappearing through a set of French doors on the opposite end of the kitchen. I squint. They must lead to the living room. The hulking shapes of a sofa and chairs are barely visible in the darkness. There's a soft *thump* as Hope drops onto the cushions.

I look over my shoulder. I left the basement door open, and I can just make out its rectangular outline in the darkness. I should leave now. Hope is passed out on the sofa. But something holds me in place. I hear Elijah's voice in the back of my head.

It's not easy to do the right thing.

My hands have started to sweat. There are two doors to the left of the fridge. I try the first one—pantry. Boxes of cereal and flour stare out at me from the shadowy darkness. Exhaling, I ease it closed again.

I'm not sure what I'm looking for, exactly. A spot of blood? Something Pastor Joe might've used to hit Hope with? I turn in place, letting the light catch every dusty corner of the kitchen. I see some dirty dishes, and a stack of old magazines, but that's all.

I lower my hand to the second doorknob. . . .

"Lost lamb," a voice murmurs.

I whirl around a second before the overhead light flicks on. White gleams off the stainless steel appliances. I cringe and shield my eyes.

"Brooklyn?" Pastor Joe stands behind me, wearing pajama pants and a plaid robe and holding a baseball bat. His crooked smile reminds me of the jack-o'-lanterns on the street. Vacant and haunting.

I back up against the wall, my shoulders going tense. "I didn't mean—"

But Pastor Joe leans the baseball bat against the fridge, relief crossing his face. "You scared me half to death. I thought you were a burglar."

I open my mouth. And then close it again. I have no idea what to say.

"Well, sit," Pastor Joe says, motioning to one of the bar stools by the center island. He peeks into the darkened room where Hope disappeared. "I see that you've returned my daughter to me. Why don't you let me make you a cup of tea to perk you up before you head home?"

He pulls the glass doors to the living room shut before I can answer, closing the two of us in the kitchen. Alone. He pulls a cupboard door open and begins rummaging around inside. Then, pushing the door closed with his elbow, he carries a random assortment of tea boxes over to the island.

I still haven't moved away from the wall.

"Sit, please," Pastor Joe says, flipping the boxes around so I can see the flavors. Honey Lemon. Cinnamon Apple Spice. Sleepytime. "Do you take milk and sugar?"

"Black is fine," I manage.

"As God intended," Pastor Joe says with another wide, fake smile. He switches a burner on with a flick of his wrist. Orange flames leap from the stove, crackling as he moves a red teakettle over them.

I look from Pastor Joe to the open basement door behind him, trying to calculate whether I could make it down the stairs before he caught me. Joe moves around the kitchen, humming under his breath as he pulls cups from the cupboard above the sink and spoons out of a drawer next to the fridge. He notices the open basement door and nudges it closed with his foot, cutting off my exit.

I move away from the wall and perch at the edge of a bar stool. "Is Gavin awake?" I ask.

Pastor Joe stops humming. "No, I'm afraid not."

My tongue feels like sand. I try to swallow, but there's not enough moisture in my mouth, and it just makes everything dry and sticky. "I—"

The teakettle starts to whistle. Pastor Joe lifts a finger. "Hold that thought." He takes the kettle off the burner and fills two cups with water. "Honey Lemon or Sleepytime?"

"Um, Honey Lemon?"

He plops a tea bag into my cup and slides it across the island. "Have you ever heard the story of the lake of fire, Brooklyn?"

I shake my head, wrapping my hands around the warm porcelain.

Pastor Joe dunks his tea bag into his own cup, staring at a spot on the wall just behind my head. "Hell is described in only a few places in the Bible. Often, it's referred to as a lake of fire. Other times it's compared to a fiery furnace."

I take a sip of tea, burning my tongue.

"In the Lord's final revelation to John, the end of the world is described as a great battle between good and evil. Christians won't be part of this, of course. Good Christians will be raptured up to heaven while, on earth, a great Beast will lead a battle against Jesus himself. Jesus will speak the Truth, and the Truth will destroy the Beast. And then the Beast, and everyone who does not believe, will be thrown into a lake of fire. Alive. To burn for all of eternity."

Pastor Joe calmly lifts his tea to his mouth, staring at me over the rim of his cup. I take another drink of my own tea, hoping it will calm my nerves.

"Why are you telling me this?" I ask, swallowing.

"I thought you should know that it's not a peaceful God I serve," Pastor Joe says, placing his cup back on the island. "It's a vengeful, violent one."

My hands feel cold, all of a sudden, even pressed against the hot mug. I look down. Steam rises from my tea, fogging my eyesight.

"Where's Gavin?" I ask. The words feel big and clumsy against my tongue. I open my mouth, wide, stretching the corners of my lips. Something's wrong.

"Gavin is staying at the hospital with Laura tonight," Pastor Joe says, taking another drink of tea. "But we had a little talk earlier. About your relationship."

I think of the look Pastor Joe gave me at the hospital. *We must remember to keep our minds and bodies pure.*

I slide off my bar stool, my knees knocking together. "Talk?"

"Gavin told me you tried to seduce him. He's worried about you." Pastor Joe's eyes flit to the French doors on the other side of the kitchen. I can just make out the silhouette of Hope's sleeping body through the glass.

"And now you're spending time with my daughter. You must've realized by now that she's . . . troubled."

The floor lurches. I prop my hand against the island to hold myself up, but my arms aren't working right. It's like there're no bones inside of them. My hand slips, and my elbow slams against the island.

"That'll be the ketamine," Pastor Joe says, standing. "You might want to—"

I don't hear the rest of his sentence. My legs collapse beneath me, and then I'm on the ground, the linoleum hard beneath my head. I blink, trying to get my eyesight to clear, but everything seems dark and far away.

Pastor Joe leans over me. "I see the sin in you, just as I saw the sin in my daughter," he says. "I won't let you work your wickedness on my son."

CHAPTER FOURTEEN

I wake up with my head hanging forward, my chin resting against my chest. Long, slow waves of pain crash over me. It's like slamming into a wall, or falling, or both at the same time. Something hard presses into my back, forcing my spine rod straight.

I lift my head and open my eyes. Everything blurs. I can just make out white carpet beneath my bare feet and white curtains pulled closed over a window on the far wall. The room is dim, lit only by a single lamp, and hulking furniture casts deep shadows across the floor. Duct tape binds my wrists to a chair. I try to wriggle my hands free, but that twists the tape into a skinny cord that digs deeper into my skin.

A hand drops onto my head. "Keep still, my child," Pastor Joe says. He stands directly behind me. I can't see him.

Stay calm, I tell myself. *Think*. Pastor Joe might be a fucking psychopath, but he's not a big guy, and he doesn't seem to have thought this out too well. I can take him.

Pastor Joe removes his hand from my head, and I hear the muffled sound of footsteps. I crane my head around to look at him, but he stands just outside my line of vision. I catch a glimpse of white hair, the frayed edge of a T-shirt.

The rest of the room spins—the ketamine rushing through my veins—then comes slowly into focus. White dressers. White bed, covered in fluffy white pillows. Angels crowd every available surface: fat cherubs holding harps, and beautiful women with golden curls and soft, feathery wings. Tall angels and short angels, all watching me with glassy, unseeing eyes.

Hope's guitar case leans against the wall next to the closet, stickers plastered across it. One of them shows a tiny ghost holding a sign that reads FEAR ME, I'M CUTE. It's the only thing in the entire room that looks like her.

"Look," I say, swallowing. My mouth feels like it's stuffed full of wool. "I was just dropping Hope off—"

Pastor Joe begins to hum, cutting me off. It takes me a moment to recognize the tune.

Amazing grace, how sweet the sound . . .

The humming grows louder, until it's directly behind me. I twist in my chair, pulling at the duct tape around my wrists. The twisty cords bite into my skin.

Pastor Joe walks around to the front of my chair and kneels. His mouth is a hard line. His white hair is mussed and sticks up at strange angles. In the dim light, his eyes look almost black.

I blink, and his face goes fuzzy, then comes into focus again. He's holding an angel statuette in one hand. This one isn't pretty. She has an unforgiving expression on her tiny porcelain face. Each feather in her wings comes to a sharp point.

"It's okay, Brooklyn," Pastor Joe says. "I don't want to hurt you."

Like hell, I think. You don't drug a teenage girl and tie her to a chair if all you're looking for is a little chat. I shift my eyes to the left and to the right, but the ketamine is still in my system. Everything blurs.

"Then whadda you want?" I ask. The drugs make my tongue feel too big inside my mouth.

"Just to talk a little. About your relationship with my son." Pastor Joe points at me with one dagger-sharp wing. "Can we do that?"

"Is this how you talk to all of your son's girlfriends?" I mumble.

Pastor Joe tilts his head to the side. He runs a finger along the sharp edge of the angel's wing. "I was hoping to pull you aside at church, to have a rational discussion about the importance of keeping your body pure. But then Gavin told me that you and Hope went to a party tonight, and I knew it was too late for that." Pastor Joe's mouth curves into a sad smile. "My daughter has a way of getting people to do exactly what she wants them to do. She gets inside their heads. Corrupts them."

"You're crazy," I spit. There doesn't seem to be any point to being polite anymore. "Hope told me everything. I know you've been beating her. I saw the bruises."

Pastor Joe grabs a handful of my hair and yanks my head back. Pain shoots up my neck. He holds the angel's wing to my cheek.

"What, exactly, did she tell you?" he asks, calmly.

"Go to hell," I spit.

There's a sharp slash down my cheek, hot as fire. I grit my teeth against the pain. The metallic scent of blood fills the air around me. I stretch my jaw. A drop of blood slides from my cheek, landing on the fluffy white carpet between my toes.

Pastor Joe lets go of my hair, and my head lolls forward. He rests the angel's wing against his chin, smearing my blood over his skin. "Don't make me use this again. I'm just trying to help you."

I force my mouth into a grim smile. I won't give him the pleasure of seeing me in pain. "Don't do me any favors."

Pastor Joe whips his hand across my face, and my head snaps painfully to the side. Lights flash before my eyes. Something thick and metallic gathers in the back of my throat.

"The Lord gives all of us burdens we must bear," he murmurs, almost to himself. "Mine is one of punishment. It's my duty to watch over his flock."

The ketamine seems to be wearing off a bit, but I still feel strangely heavy and slow. I spit blood onto the white carpet. "Like you watched over your own daughter?"

"You're talking about something you know nothing about."

"Enlighten me, then."

Pastor Joe stares at me for a long moment, the dim light reflected in his black eyes. "My Hope was a light in the darkness of this world. She was a beacon, leading the lost toward Christ. I brought her and her brother along with me on my missionary trips when she was little. Gavin was always a good little boy, but not like Hope. She spread hope to whomever she met. That's where her name comes from." Pastor Joe stands, dropping the bloody angel to the floor. "*Esperanza. Nadzieja. Amal.* I used to know that word in every language. People would see my little girl, and 'hope' would spring from their lips. Like a miracle."

"Charming," I say, through gritted teeth.

"Then, as she grew older, something changed. A darkness took hold. She became quiet. Grim."

"Sounds like she turned into a normal teenage girl."

Pastor Joe ignores me. He walks around behind my chair. "People no longer spoke of 'hope' when they saw her. They said another word, instead. *Barabas. Balakyot. Diablo.*"

"So you're telling me this has nothing to do with Hope sleeping with your son?"

Pastor Joe's shoulders stiffen, but when he speaks his voice is calm. "I was meeting with another pastor that night. I'd hoped to exorcise the demon from Hope before any real damage could occur. But when I got back, I saw that she'd already seduced Gavin. Her own brother. If I hadn't intervened, the demon would have taken him, too."

"And Gavin is blameless in all this?"

"Gavin was seduced by evil, as we are all seduced. I'd hoped to keep him away from her. But I failed him then. I won't fail him now, with you."

Pastor Joe starts humming again.

Amazing grace, how sweet the sound . . .

I curl my toes into the carpet. The humming is in my ear, but I can't tell if it's because Pastor Joe is leaning toward me, or if the acoustics in the small room make him seem louder, closer. I cringe, imagining I can feel his breath on my skin.

My chair tilts backward. I wrap my fingers around the seat, pressing them into the wood. Splinters drive into the tender skin beneath my nails. Pastor Joe begins to drag my chair across the room.

"What are you doing?" I ask. He doesn't answer. He stops beside a door on the far wall and stands my chair upright.

"My daughter has corrupted you, as she tried to corrupt her brother. But don't worry. I won't let your soul be lost."

He fumbles in his pocket for something—keys. I hear the metal clank together as he pulls them out and fits them into a lock in the door. There's a click, and he pulls the door open. I twist my head around, but I can't see. Pastor Joe pockets the keys and then pulls my chair in front of the room. I turn to look inside. . . .

It's a closet, barely large enough for a person. Knives jut away from the walls and the door, some twisted and curved, others long and thick, like oversized nails. Dried blood and rust crusts around the blades.

Oh God. He put Hope in that room. He's going to put *me* in that room.

"Let me go, you sick fuck!" I scream.

"I really wish we were doing this at the church. That's where I keep all my best tools. But God tells us to make do with what we have." Pastor Joe crouches behind me, unwinding the duct tape from my wrists. Sharp pain jolts through my arms as the tape peels the hair off my skin.

"You can't do this," I choke out.

"Physical pain brings us closer to God," Pastor Joe says. He rips a piece of duct tape away, and I'm able to wriggle my hand free. "You'll see. I'll—"

I lurch forward, throwing my elbow back against Pastor Joe's face. I feel it connect with his chin. He swears, letting go of my hand. *Yes.* I twist around in the chair, trying to pull my opposite hand free.

Pastor Joe cracks his fist against my knee. Something crunches, and I fall to the ground. I cry out, and tears spring to my eyes. I never knew a knee could hurt so badly. It feels wrong. Like my bones have shifted out of place and are rattling around below my skin. I think of marbles flopping around in a sock, and another sharp stab of pain shoots up my leg.

He grabs me by the shoulders and stands me upright, one hand still attached to the chair with a strip of duct tape. He backs me into the closet, using his other hand to rip the tape away. The chair falls back onto the floor.

I try, again, to shove my way past him, and he punches me—hard—in the stomach. All of the air leaves my body in a sudden rush. It feels like my gut has split open beneath his fist. I imagine blood spreading just below the surface of my skin.

I stumble backward, and a sharp point drives into the skin next to my spine. I scream and lurch forward— another blade catches me under the ribs.

"Be still," Pastor Joe warns. He has one hand propped on the door and he's pushing it closed. I reach for the crack in the door, the one last blade-free space, but Pastor Joe is too quick. He closes the door, and I'm all alone, blades winking in the darkness around me.

CHAPTER FIFTEEN

I can't see the blades in the dark, but I feel them hovering centimeters from my skin. I'm afraid to move my hands away from my sides.

"Help!" I try to scream, but my voice comes out sounding thin. I'm too nervous to inhale any deeper, worried the blades will nick my chest or stomach. I press my lips together, imagining Hope asleep on the couch. She wouldn't hear me, anyway.

I don't know how long I stay frozen like that. It feels like hours, but it could be minutes. Time doesn't make sense inside that tiny black box. Sweat rolls down my forehead, leaving my skin itchy and damp, but I don't dare raise my hand to wipe it away. A dull ache forms in my left hip, and I start to shift my weight to the right— but then I picture a razor-sharp blade sliding into my leg, ripping through my skin, and I force myself upright again. My leg wobbles beneath me.

Pull yourself together, Brooklyn. I'm not getting out of here if I start panicking now.

I concentrate on breathing in and out, in and out, like I'm in a yoga class from hell. I close my eyes and focus on the air filling my lungs. It seems thinner than it was in Hope's room, but I can't tell if there's really less oxygen or if I feel light-headed because I'm losing blood.

Throbbing pain moves through my gut, reminding me of the stab wound just below my ribs. I want to touch it, to see how deep it is, but fear keeps me still. I imagine blood oozing past the ragged edges of my skin, gathering in the waistband of my jeans. I don't know how much longer I have before my legs give out and I collapse onto the jagged knives in front of me. I feel weak. Any second now, I'll stumble.

"Please," I whisper. I don't know who I'm talking to. Myself, maybe. *Keep standing. Stay strong. I won't let this sick freak get the best of me.*

My knee buckles, and I sway backward. A blade slices through my T-shirt, nicking the skin on my back. I gasp, forcing myself still.

A floorboard creaks on the other side of the closet

door. I'm suddenly alert. The pain in my leg and my gut fades to the back of my head. My muscles tense.

Open the door, asshole, I think. If he thinks I'm going to cower in here all weak and scared, he's got another think coming.

My breath sounds ragged and loud in the silent space. My heartbeat is a slow, steady drum. I flex my fingers, waiting. Seconds stretch into minutes. My muscles relax. I heard wrong. There's no one there.

Then—a click of metal as the door is unlocked. A sliver of dim, golden light appears. It hurts my eyes, and I shrink backward. A dozen blades prick my back at the same moment, forcing me upright again.

Pastor Joe pulls the door all the way open. "Have you enjoyed the sinner's room, Brooklyn?" he asks.

For a moment I forget that I'm a skinny teenage girl and he's a full-grown man.

I hurl my body forward, colliding with him, and the two of us tumble to the ground in a tangled mess of arms and legs. I push myself off him and scramble to my feet. I race for the door, ignoring the pain shooting through my legs and the lingering effects of the ketamine making my body slow and clumsy.

Almost there. Just a few more steps . . .

Pastor Joe grabs my ankle and pulls. My leg slides out from under me, and I drop to my knees, groaning.

"Help!" I shout at the top of my lungs, hoping to wake

Hope. An angel topples off her dresser and smashes against the floor, spraying the carpet with tiny shards of porcelain.

"Hold still," Pastor Joe mutters. I roll onto my back, kicking at his face, but he grabs my other leg before I make contact. He yanks me forward, and my head slams into the floor. Lights flash across my eyes. I blink, and Pastor Joe is leaning over me. On instinct, I curl my fingers into a claw and rake them across his face. I feel the skin give way beneath my nails and smile. *Got him.*

He reels backward. "Bitch!"

I go to scratch him again, but he grabs my arm, holding me down. "Hope!" I scream, again. "Someone! *Please.*"

He cracks his fist across my cheekbone, and my head whips to the side. My skull explodes with white light. I'm dimly aware that I need to get up, I need to *fight*, but he hit me too hard. My entire body feels numb.

Pastor Joe stands, groaning. I tell my arms to move but they just twitch, uselessly, at my sides. He bends over my motionless body and takes me by the wrists.

My eyelids droop. I'm about to lose consciousness. *Stay awake!* I scream at myself. But it's no use. I can't lift my head or my arm. I can't move my legs.

Grunting, Pastor Joe drags me out of Hope's room and down the hall. The floor beneath me changes from carpet to something cold and hard. Light flickers behind my closed lids—candles, I think.

I force my eyes back open. Cream-colored tile and a bathtub the size of a swimming pool. Dark cabinets covered in tall white candles. A framed picture of a grassy field thick with wildflowers. *He maketh me to lie down in green pastures*, it reads.

The room blurs. I feel dizzy. I concentrate all my energy on keeping my eyes open. I can't pass out now. If I pass out, I'm dead.

Pastor Joe lets go of my arms. I wait until he steps away from my body, and then I roll onto my side, groaning.

"Don't make me tie you up again," he says from above me. I hesitate . . . then nod, one cheek still pressed to the cold tile. I couldn't outrun him right now, even if I did have the energy to stand. I'll have to wait.

Pastor Joe moves around the bathroom. I can't see what he's doing without lifting my head, so I watch the candlelight flicker over the tile. A folded piece of cloth sits beside a glass bottle that's so dirty I can't see what's inside. I consider them both, trying to figure out what he's planning next. Whatever it is, it's going to hurt.

I wiggle my fingers and my toes to make sure everything is still working. They move on my command, and I exhale, relieved.

Pastor Joe grabs me by the shoulders and hoists me into a sitting position. I let my body go loose and floppy, so he'll think I'm still weak. He leans me against the bathtub. A belt dangles from his hand, the rough leather worn smooth and shiny in places from years of handling. I stare at the belt, horror rising inside me. Every muscle inside of me tenses, longing to fight.

Pastor Joe loops the belt around my shoulders, strapping my arms close to my body. Leather snaps, echoing in the tiled room. "I take no pleasure in this, Brooklyn." He stands and shuffles to the other side of the bathroom. "But I was soft on Hope at first, and I regret that now, every day."

I moan as I test the straps. They're loose enough.

"Maybe if I'd exorcised her early enough, before the demon took hold, she could've been saved," he continues.

I wait until his back is turned, and then I wriggle beneath the belt. It slides down to my elbows. If I get it down a bit farther, I'll get one arm free.

Pastor Joe turns back around. I go still.

"Have you been baptized, Brooklyn?" he asks. I shake my head. "I assumed as much. Baptism is a beautiful thing. It makes you clean in the eyes of the Lord. It washes away all of your past sins."

He kneels beside me, removing the folded cloth from the floor. "This is the prayer cloth given to me by the pastor I met with that night in South America." He unfolds the cloth, slowly, as he speaks. "He was an expert in all manner of sin. He could tell by looking at someone whether the devil was at work in their soul."

Pastor Joe drapes the cloth over both hands, holding it out in front of me. The fabric must've been a brilliant blue, once, but now it's a nappy gray color. Pastor Joe handles it like it's something holy. I bet he never thought to wash it.

"The devil is seducing you, Brooklyn. But there's still time." He leans closer to me, pulling the cloth tight between his hands. "Are you strong enough to fight him off?"

I stare at the cloth. Now that I look closer, I realize it isn't dirt clinging to the fabric. It's blood. I swallow, looking back up at Pastor Joe. "I—"

He twists the bloody cloth around my face before I can finish. I inhale on instinct—and then start choking. The cloth smells like dirt and overcooked meat. My eyes fill with tears at the stench.

"Shhh . . . ," Pastor Joe murmurs, tying the cloth tighter around my head. "Be calm. We're going to baptize you."

The scent creeps up my nose and down my throat. It's suffocating. I try not to inhale, but fear is making me hyperventilate.

This isn't the first time he's done this, I realize. He's done it to Hope, too. My chest rises and falls rapidly as I suck down short bursts of stinking, rancid air.

Be still, I tell myself, even as every muscle inside my body clenches. I need to save myself before I worry about Hope. I wriggle beneath the leather belt, shifting it down a little farther. . . .

Pastor Joe shuffles around the bathroom, his shoes squeaking over the tile. There's a sound like a bottle being uncorked. And then—

Water hits my face, quickly soaking the prayer cloth covering my mouth and nose. It's *putrid*. Like sewer water. I clench my lips shut and it pours down my nose instead, burning the back of my throat. I try to inhale, and the wet cloth flutters over my nostrils, making it impossible to breathe.

I curl my knees toward my chest, but Pastor Joe grabs my ankles, wrenching my legs straight again.

"Struggling will only make this hurt more," he says. I kick again, but Pastor Joe is too strong. He curls his hands around my ankles, holding me down. My mouth flops open, gasping.

Pastor Joe releases my legs just long enough to throw more water at my face. It slams into me like a punch. My vision swims. Deep, hacking coughs rattle my chest. I feel like I'm drowning. I twist beneath the belt. It slides down past my elbows.

Pastor Joe is speaking, but it takes me a moment to work out what he's saying. "I baptize this child in the name of the Father, the Son, and—"

More water hits my face. I feel it in my mouth and throat and lungs. My skull fills with stinking, rancid water. I try, again, to breathe, but there's no air left. Only water and the stinking, dirty cloth covering my mouth. With the last of my strength, I yank my arm upward. The belt digs into my skin, holding it in place.

I'm going to die here, I realize, horrified. *I'm going to die right now.*

No. I won't go like this. Violently, desperately, I wrench at my shoulder, and this time, my arm slips free. I claw at the air in front of me, and my fingers dig into soft flesh. Something moist oozes beneath my nails.

Pastor Joe screams, but I don't let go. I dig deeper. Blood and flesh well up beneath my fingernails, but still, I hold on. Pastor Joe's screams grow louder—desperate. He tries to jerk away from me, but I won't release my grip. I claw and scratch at his skin until, finally, I feel something *tear*. Then, I let go.

I unwind the cloth from my face with trembling fingers. *Faster*, I think. I rip the cloth away from my face, gasping for air.

Pastor Joe crouches on the bathroom floor, moaning. Blood pools beneath his face. I fumble with the belt buckle, my fingers thick and shaking. It clatters to the floor. I'm free.

I push myself to my feet and hurry across the room, but my legs are still weak. I lurch to the side, bumping into a cupboard covered in flickering candles. A few of the candles topple over, rolling to the floor.

"Brooklyn?" Pastor Joe moans. I hesitate as he lifts his face.

The skin at the corner of his lip has been torn wide. His mouth gapes open, the teeth below slicked with blood. Deep claw marks have shredded his gums and chin. Ragged flaps of skin hang from his bones, like scraps of fabric. It looks like hamburger meat, red and raw.

Chunks of vomit rise in my throat as I stare at him. He crawls toward me, but I don't think he sees me. His eyes have gone cloudy, blinded with pain.

"Don't leave me like this," he begs. "Please. Don't let the devil win."

I pull open the bathroom door and hurry into the hall. There's a padlock connected to the doorframe— just like the one on Hope's closet. I reach up and slam it closed, relief flooding my chest when I hear the metal lock slide into place. I lean against the door, breathing in deep.

I'm safe. He can't get out of the bathroom now.

I inhale again, relishing the fresh air filling my lungs. I step away from the door, and that's when I smell it. Smoke. I turn back around.

Smoke trickles out from the crack below the bathroom door, quickly filling the hall around me.

CHAPTER SIXTEEN

I stand outside the bathroom, adrenaline pumping through my veins. I curl my hands into fists. It's not enough just to lock Pastor Joe inside his own bathroom. I want to hurt him, like he hurt me. Like he hurt Hope. I want to hear him scream.

Smoke billows out from the crack below the door. It's thick and gray—almost black. The smell crawls up my nose and stings my eyes. The candle fire must have caught onto something. A tear spills onto my cheek, but I don't look away. I picture the fire eating away what's left of Pastor Joe's face. Making his skin bubble. My lips curl into a shaky grin. *Good.*

A fist slams against the door, making the wood vibrate. I look at the padlock. It trembles. But it holds.

"Brooklyn?" Pastor Joe says. His voice is faint, and he releases a deep, phlegmy cough. "Brooklyn, are you still out there?"

I'm out here all right, you sick fuck. I curl my hands into fists. Every cut in my skin flares, reminding me what he did to me. What he's done to others. I stare at the door without saying a word.

"Brooklyn?" Pastor Joe tries again. His voice sounds fainter now. "Please. The candle . . ."

He starts coughing again, and for a long moment, he can't seem to speak. I creep closer to the door, blood slick against the bottoms of my feet.

"Can't put out the fire . . . ," Pastor Joe chokes out. "Can't see . . . too much smoke."

I raise a hand to the bathroom door. It feels warm beneath my fingers. Smoke seeps out from the cracks, curling around my feet and making the air in the hallway hazy. It's getting harder to breathe.

Pastor Joe pounds against the door again, but I don't flinch.

"If . . . leave . . . I'll . . . die . . ."

"You *deserve* to die," I say.

For a long moment there's quiet. I press my ear to the wood so I can hear what's happening.

"Maybe . . . ," he murmurs, and I can tell the smoke is getting to him. He doesn't have much longer. "But do you really . . . want to be the one who killed me?"

I hesitate. If I let him die, I can't call the police. I can't report what he did to me. But Hope said he's friends with the police. They wouldn't believe me, anyway.

Another thought flashes through my head. *If he's dead, he can't hurt her anymore.*

There's a sound like metal scraping against wood. I glance at the crack beneath the bathroom door. Silver glints up at me as Pastor Joe pushes a tiny key into the hall, inches from my bare feet.

Flecks of blood stain my toes, reminding me that Pastor Joe tortured me. For hours. A man like that doesn't deserve to live.

But he's right. I don't want to be a murderer, either.

"Please . . . ," Pastor Joe murmurs. "Can't breathe . . ."

Smoke fills my mouth, making me dizzy. I can't think straight. My eyes won't stop watering. This choice shouldn't be up to me. I should leave it in the hands of God, or fate, or whatever force is out there controlling us. If there really is a God, and he wants to save the sadistic pastor, he'll show him the way out.

"You still alive in there, asshole?" I shout, banging on the door. No one answers.

I kneel and pick the key up off the floor, fitting it into the padlock. Here goes nothing. I turn, and the padlock pops open.

I stare at the door for a long moment, waiting for Pastor Joe to open it, eyes manic, lips curled into a horrifying smile. But the door doesn't move. Maybe I was too late.

I toss the padlock onto the floor. There's a heavy thud as it slides over the wood. I *hope* I was too late.

I back toward the staircase. And then I turn and run. I don't look back. Not when I reach the bottom of the stairs or hurry into the kitchen. Smoke pours down the stairs after me, making the air thick and hot. I hesitate next to the French doors that lead to the living room. I can see Hope's body in the darkness behind the glass, still sleeping. I reach for the door.

Something crashes against the floor upstairs. Every muscle in my body goes tense, and my mouth fills with the taste of something sick and sour. Pastor Joe. I throw the door open and race into the living room.

"Hope, wake up!" I shout. Hope murmurs something, sleepily, but her eyes stay shut. I glance over my shoulder, half expecting to see Pastor Joe stomping down the stairs behind me. The air is already thick and hazy with smoke.

"Hope!" I shake her, and when she doesn't wake up, I grab her below the shoulders and pull. She's tiny, and

I easily drag her out the front door and onto the porch.
Smoke pours from the windows of the house, rising into
the night sky like a beacon.

I collapse next to her, gasping for breath. It takes a
long moment to cough the smoke from my lungs.

She's groaning now, her expression twisting as she
starts to wake. I hesitate. If she sees me here when she
wakes up, I'll have to explain what her father did to me.
What I did to him.

I pull my legs beneath me, trying to gather the energy
to stand again. Hope starts to cough. I stand, racing down
the stairs and into the bushes. I glance back through the
leaves. Hope's fully awake now. She watches the smoke
overtake her house with a look of horror on her face.

Guilt twists inside of me. A better person would go to
her, comfort her. But I just duck farther into the bushes,
where I'm sure she won't see me.

Once I've caught my breath I start the long walk
home.

I head straight for the laundry room and strip down,
shoving every bit of clothing directly into the washing
machine. I add too much soap and set the machine to
heavy duty, hoping that'll be enough to scrub away all
the smoke and blood and dirt. For a long moment I just
stand there, naked, watching my clothes spin and twirl

behind the glass. In just an hour, they'll be clean. And it will be like this night never happened.

The sun isn't up yet, but the sky has turned a lighter shade of blue. My parents will wake up soon. I slip into the downstairs shower and quickly scrub the grime from my skin. The bar of soap is black when I'm finished, so I spend another few minutes washing that, too. By the time I switch off the faucet, everything's good as new. I grab pajamas from a fresh load in the laundry room, pull them on, and yank my hair back in my standard braids.

I rub the condensation from the mirror and stare at my reflection. The skin around my wrists is red from the duct tape, but my pajamas cover the rest of the cuts and bruises on my body. A long, thin scratch cuts across my face, violently red against my pale skin.

I can't tell the police what happened tonight. What I did. Which means I can't tell anyone. I touch the edges of the scratch on my face, cringing at the sudden flare of pain. Mom and Dad might miss my other wounds—but they're going to notice that one. I'll have to come up with a really good lie.

I tug at the sleeves of my pajamas and stare into my own eyes. They look hollow and haunted, and dark circles shade the skin below them. It'll be fine, I tell myself. I can blame it on nightmares if anybody asks. It wouldn't even be a lie. What happened tonight was a nightmare.

I creep upstairs and down the hall, casting one glance at my parents' bedroom to make sure I haven't woken them up. Their door is closed. Breathing a sigh of relief, I slip into my own room and hurriedly shut the door.

It was a nightmare, I think, again, leaning my forehead against the cool wood. Just a nightmare.

The smell of burning skin clings to my nostrils, and, despite my shower, I can still feel blood on my hands and feet. Between my fingers. Under my toenails.

I crawl into bed and roll onto my side, the mattress creaking beneath me. As much as I want to pretend that what happened tonight was just a nightmare, it wasn't. It was real, and tomorrow, things are going to be very different—one way or another. Before I close my eyes, I grab my phone and pull up Gavin's number. I have to do one more thing before I go to sleep.

Hope told me everything, I write. **We're done.**

I press send, and then I turn my phone off and force my eyes closed. I don't want to read his response.

Wind howls against my bedroom window, sounding just like a scream. I replay that moment outside the bathroom door again and again. Pastor Joe begging me to help him. His voice going quiet the second before I unlocked the padlock. I shiver and roll over in bed.

I don't know what would be worse. If he survived, and he's out in the dark right now, plotting his revenge.

Or if he burned to ash, surrounded by his instruments of pain.

The wind picks up. It rattles my window, shaking the frame so hard that the glass creaks. I pull a pillow over my head to block the sound. But the howling is too loud. It echoes through my head.

Then, just below the scream of the wind—*tap tap tap*.

My eyes pop open. With the pillow over my head, everything around me is dark. I count the beating of my heart, focusing on the steady thud to calm my nerves. Silence. And then, again—*tap tap tap*.

I sit up, tossing my pillow to the floor. The tapping is coming from the window. I place one foot on the cold, wooden floor, and then the other.

Tap tap tap.

I ease to my feet. *It's a tree branch*, I tell myself. The huge oak tree in the yard is just outside my window. The wind is going crazy, sending it bumping into the glass, and I'm already freaked out, so I've convinced myself that it's something more. Something sinister. I creep across my room, my eyes never leaving the window. My gauzy white curtains cover the glass, but I see shadows moving beyond them.

Tree branches, I tell myself again. *Maybe a squirrel.*

Tap tap tap.

I reach forward, fingers trembling, and grab a handful

of curtain. For a moment I just stand there. Frozen. And then I jerk the curtain away.

Pastor Joe stands outside. Grinning. Meaty bits of eyeball trail down his cheek. His eye socket is red and hollow and leaking blood. The other half of his face has been burned. I can smell the thick, charred scent of burning meat through the glass.

He opens his mouth and screams.

I jerk awake, Pastor Joe's scream still ringing in my ears. I throw back my comforter and scramble out of bed, cringing the second I place weight on my legs. My body hasn't recovered from my night in the sinner's room. My knees shake as I cross the room.

I grab my phone off my bedside table and turn it on again. I've only been asleep for a few hours, but it's possible that there's already an update on the fire. I quickly look up *Fire Friend Mississippi Pastor Joe*. Biting down on my lower lip, I scan through the results. They all say the same thing.

Fire in the sleepy town of Friend, Mississippi . . .

. . . beloved local pastor found dead.

I swear under my breath. That's it, then. He's really gone. I close out of the browser window and find Hope's name in my contact list.

I saw the news, I type. **Where are you?**

I stare at the screen for a long time. But Hope doesn't respond.

CHAPTER SEVENTEEN

My legs are jittery. I can't stop tapping my foot and bouncing my knee. I wrap my arms around my chest, rubbing my hands up and down the skin between my wrist and elbow until it feels raw and itchy. I must look crazy, like a meth addict waiting for my next fix. I have to do something to distract myself.

I throw on a pair of jeans and a T-shirt and head down to the kitchen.

"Mom?" I call, rounding the corner. The tile feels cold against my bare feet, even though the air in the kitchen is thick and muggy. My T-shirt sticks to my back with sweat. "I'm not feeling well, so I think I'm going to stay home sick today."

There's a Post-it note on the fridge: *Gone to store.* I pluck it off with two fingers, frowning.

The doorbell rings, making me flinch. I drop the Post-it and it flutters halfway to the floor before getting caught on my pajama pants. I stare down at it for a long moment.

The doorbell rings again.

I hold my breath as I cross the kitchen and poke my head into the hallway. I picture cops on my front steps. Police officers in stiff blue uniforms, guns hanging from their belts, notepads in their hands. I think about the fact that I already have a few warnings for shoplifting and protesting. They'll have questions about Pastor Joe. Somehow, they'll figure out what I did.

"Don't be stupid," I whisper into the empty hallway. There's no way they could know.

I head down the hall and pull open the front door. Elijah stands on the porch, his bike helmet propped beneath one arm. His hair is plastered to his head with sweat.

"What are you doing here?" I blurt. Elijah gives me a look, and I mentally kick myself. *Be cool.* "Sorry. I just wasn't expecting you."

"Yeah. Well, I wanted to stop by." Elijah leans against the wooden railing surrounding our porch. "You left a little quickly last night."

I touch my lips with one finger. "I remember."

"I guess that's a good sign." Elijah studies something on my face, frowning. I touch my cheek and cringe, remembering a dagger-sharp angel's wing covered in blood. The cut is still tender.

"I . . . uh, think I scratched myself in my sleep," I mutter, tilting my head so that Elijah can't get a closer look at the cut. "I guess my fingernails are too long."

Elijah narrows his eyes. "I thought only infants did that."

"Apparently not." I lean against the door. All at once, my entire body starts to ache. I'm aware of every cut Pastor Joe left on me, and every nick from every knife inside the sinner's room. I feel like shredded tissue paper. It's amazing that my skin can still hold me together.

How am I supposed to explain what happened last night to Elijah? To *anyone*?

I lift my hand to my face, pinching the bridge of my nose between two fingers. My sleeve slides down to my elbow, revealing the raw skin circling my wrist. Elijah looks from my wrist to the scratch on my cheek.

I tug the sleeve back over my hand, but he pushes himself away from the bannister and grabs me by the elbow, jerking my arm between us. Angry red skin glares up at me. I swallow and look away, focusing on the trees behind Elijah's head. I don't need to be reminded.

"Brooklyn," Elijah says in a low voice. "What happened?"

I try to pull my arm away from him, but he holds tight. "It's nothing—"

A step creaks, and we both flinch. Gavin stands on the porch stairs, glaring up at us. His eyes shift to my hand, which Elijah is still holding. Elijah drops it and takes an awkward step away from me.

"What the hell, Brooklyn?" Gavin asks. I stiffen, but there's no avoiding him. I guess we're doing this now.

"Can you give us a second, Elijah?" I ask.

Elijah hesitates. He glances at Gavin and then back at me again. "Yeah. Okay. I guess it's none of my business."

I clasp my hand around my arm, my thumb brushing against the still tender skin. "That's not what I—"

But Elijah's already down the steps and rounding the corner. Gavin watches him go, his body tense.

"You broke up with me with a text?" he says once we're alone. His mouth twists, but his eyes stay hard. "You have no idea what the last few hours have been like for me. I needed you."

His eyes are rimmed with red, the skin around his nostrils raw and dry. This isn't about us. Obviously. He just found out his father died.

"I'm sorry about your dad," I say, carefully. "But after what Hope told me, I don't think I'm the right person for you to talk to."

I back inside the house and start to pull the door shut. Gavin takes the porch steps two at a time and slides his hand between the door and the frame.

"What did she say to you?" he asks, yanking the door back open. "Because she manipulates people. You can't trust her."

"Gavin. You're in pain. I don't want to do this right now—"

"Don't you walk away from me!" Gavin screams. He starts to pace, but the porch is small and there's only room for him to take three steps in each direction. I hesitate at the door. If anyone else dumped her boyfriend on the same day his dad died, it'd be monstrous. But how could I be expected to spend one more day with Gavin, knowing what he did?

"Maybe you should call a friend," I say. "Laura, or—"

Gavin throws his fist into the wall. I hear a crunch, and a crack spreads through the siding.

I throw both hands over my mouth. Gavin cringes and clutches his hand to his chest. His knuckles are raw and bloody. He starts to pace again, not bothering to wipe the blood from his hands. It drips to the floor, specking the porch with red.

"You should go," I say.

Gavin stares down at his fist, watching the blood run over his knuckles. "I'm not giving up on us," he says. "I need you."

Sweat gathers between my fingers and the doorknob. I itch to pull it open and disappear inside.

"We're done," I say, my voice trembling. "You really need to go."

I don't hang around to make sure he leaves. Instead, I twist the dead bolt behind me. I hear Gavin's footsteps on the porch.

Thud thud. Pause. *Thud. Thud.* It sounds like he's pacing again.

Swearing, I turn back around and peer through the peephole. The fish-eye lens distorts Gavin's body, making his head too small, his arms and legs strangely long.

He stares at the door for a long moment. I half expect him to pound against the wood, demand that I come back outside and let him yell at me a little more. But he just shakes his head and hurries back down the stairs. I'm alone again. Finally.

I hurry into the kitchen to wash my hands. I still feel dirty from last night. I turn the faucet up as hot as it'll go and shove my hands beneath the water. After a few minutes, my skin feels delightfully numb. I look up, catching sight of myself in the reflection off the window above the sink.

The cut Pastor Joe left is bright red against my cheek. My braids have started to come loose, and bits of hair frizz around my face.

You're like a hot Pippi Longstocking, I hear Gavin say. The words make me cringe. Without stopping to think about what I'm doing, I pull the kitchen shears from the knife block on the counter, pinch my braid between my fingers, and—

Snip. A chunk of red hair drops into the sink, the edges instantly curling in the leftover water. I grab my other braid and—*snip*—all gone. My remaining hair sticks out from beneath my ears, jagged and uneven.

There, I think, staring at my reflection. *That feels better.*

CHAPTER EIGHTEEN

The smell of bleach hangs in the air, making my eyes water.

"Maybe we should open a window," I say, waving a hand in front of my nose.

Deirdre finger-combs my freshly cut hair. Her last class is at noon on Fridays, but I'm pretty sure she ducked out early so she'd have time to bleach my hair before her shift at Liquid.

We're facing the oversized mirror leaning against my wall, our reflections peering back at us. She's perched on the edge of my bed, while I sit between her legs, newspapers covering the floor around us.

"Don't be a baby. This is only going to take a second." Deirdre grabs the bowl filled with bleach from the floor and loads up the dye brush. "Now tilt your head back."

I lean back, holding my breath. Deirdre spreads goopy grayish cream over my head. It feels pleasantly cool against my scalp.

"So what happened with the other guy?" she asks. I just finished telling her the story of my short, doomed relationship with Gavin. A highly edited, PG-rated version of the story, at least. Rather than getting into the incest and torture, I made it seem like it was Gavin's slut shaming and prudishness that tore us apart.

To her credit, she hasn't said *I told you so*. Yet.

"Who, Elijah?" I ask. The smell of bleach creeps up my nose, making me cringe. "I texted him after Gavin left and said I needed some space."

Deirdre nods. "Bend forward so I can get the back of your head."

I tip my head toward my chest as Deirdre moves the dye brush down toward my neck. "Is this supposed to sting?"

"That means it's working."

"It's working a lot."

Low sobs echo from my laptop speakers. I glance at the screen as a man dressed like a samurai opens a switchblade with a flick of his wrist. He leans over the girl he's tied to a bed and lowers the blade to her arm.

It's *Flowers of Flesh and Blood*, the movie I've been dying to see for months. The plot revolves around this samurai dude kidnapping and drugging a woman and then slowly dismembering her body.

There's a sick, wet sound. The samurai pulls the knife through skin and bone, gleefully, while the woman sobs. Blood leaks onto the mattress. The samurai grabs the woman's fingers, separating her wrist from the rest of her arm. He pulls—

I lean forward and snap the laptop closed.

"What's that about?" Deirdre asks as I settle back in front of her.

I shrug. "It's not as good as the first one."

"Are you kidding? It's pure torture porn. You love that crap."

I press my lips together, saying nothing. It's easier to appreciate torture porn when you haven't lived through it.

"There," Deirdre says, plopping the dye brush back into the bowl. "You're all done. That wasn't so bad, was it?"

"How long do I leave it on?"

"Thirty minutes." Deirdre's eyes shift back to my laptop. "You sure you don't want to try the creepy movie again? That was our deal. You let me bleach your hair, and I try to keep my lunch down while some guy cuts his girlfriend into tiny pieces on your computer screen."

"Nah, that's okay." I picture the samurai pulling his blade through that poor girl's arm, ripping her hand clean off. I think I'm going to be sick.

I push myself to my feet and head for the door. "I'm going to check this out," I lie, stumbling into the hallway.

"It's not done yet!" Deirdre shouts after me.

I hurry into the bathroom and push the door shut behind me, pressing my body against it. I squeeze my eyes closed and count to ten—quickly first, then again, slow.

One. Pause. *Two.*

I picture Pastor Joe kneeling in front of me, gripping that ugly porcelain angel. I trace the cut he left across my skin, and my throat tightens, like someone's wrapped their fingers around my neck. I crouch over the toilet, but all I do is gasp, a veil of sweat forming beneath my goopy hair. I lean back on my heels.

Something drips behind me, echoing in the small room. I stare at the shower. A flimsy white curtain hides half the tub.

Shivers race over my skin. Anything could be hiding behind that curtain.

"There's nothing there." I feel the words rising up from my throat, but the voice that slips past my lips isn't mine. It's a trembling voice that bounces off the tile walls and echoes back at me, all faint and cowardly. I feel a hot flare of anger toward Pastor Joe.

How dare he make me weak?

Drip. Drip.

I study the shower curtain, looking for shadows moving behind the thin plastic. *Don't be an idiot. There's nothing there. It's just the bathroom. Stand up and leave. Go back to your room. Talk to Deirdre.*

I press my palms against the floor and slide my feet beneath me, taking a deep breath—

A sour, rotting scent fills my nostrils. I choke and cover my nose and mouth with both hands, my eyes watering. There's something dead in this room with me.

My hands act on their own, reaching forward and tearing the curtain back before my brain can catch up and tell me what a bad idea that is. The plastic rings that hold the curtain in place pop off the bar and clatter to the floor, pinging against my bare feet.

Dismembered arms and legs fill the tub, floating in a pool of blood the color of oil. My eyes travel over broken bones and lifeless hands. Toes with jagged nails. Muscle and tendons spilling out over the porcelain. The limbs are bloated, veins spiderwebbing over the pale skin. A maggot wiggles out from beneath a fingernail and drops into the blood.

Nestled in the middle of the decay is Pastor Joe's decapitated head. His eyes are glassy and yellow, his grinning lips purple. The side of his mouth flaps open, revealing broken, yellow teeth and blackened gums.

His fingers twitch. His eyes shift to my face.

"I see the devil at work in your soul, Brooklyn," he says in a low, raspy voice. Blood spurts from his lips. "Are you strong enough to fight him?"

I crab-crawl away from the tub, screaming until my throat feels raw.

Footsteps slam through the hallway. The door behind me swings open.

"Brooklyn?" Deirdre says, panting. "What happened? Is it the dye? Did I screw something up?"

I can't find my voice, so I point. "There. It's in the tub."

"What's in the tub?"

I look back over my shoulder. The tub is empty. Water drips from the showerhead, but it doesn't sound like water at all. It's thicker, heavier.

Like blood.

Deirdre doesn't buy my bullshit lie about seeing a spider crawl out of the drain. But she gets that I need some alone time.

"You make a killer blonde," she says, winking at me before slipping out the front door. I run a finger along one crunchy, newly bleached lock. Hair color is the last thing on my mind right now. I wave goodbye and close the door as Deirdre hurries down the porch steps.

I see the devil at work in your soul.

An icy finger touches the base of my spine. I clench my shoulders until it goes away.

I grab my cell from my room—still no text from Hope. I creep through the house, locking every window, every door. I double-check the narrow windows in the basement, the concrete cold beneath my feet as I rise to my tiptoes and try to shove the window open. It stays closed, thank God. The lock on one of the kitchen windows is loose, so I break the handle off a broom we never use anymore and wedge the window shut.

Pastor Joe is dead, I tell myself. I'm overreacting. But I still twist the dead bolt on the back door in the kitchen. I stare into the backyard. The sun is completely down now, and the only light comes from the neighbor's jack-o'-lantern. Two floating triangles and a crescent smile in the darkness.

"Oh my God!"

I throw a hand over my mouth to keep from screaming, flinging my phone across the room in the process. It smacks against the floor as I spin around to face my mom, her face white with horror.

"What? What happened?" I shout. Her face crumples. She reaches forward, pinching a strand of bleached hair between two fingers.

"What did you do to your hair?"

My heart slows to a steady pound. I shrug her hand away. "Deirdre bleached it. Don't look so scandalized."

Mom rubs a hand over her forehead, smudging dirt across her skin. She's wearing her gardening shorts, the nerdy kneepads she bought online strapped around her legs.

"I guess it'll grow back. Eventually," she says, wrinkling her nose. "I'm going to go shower and then we can figure out dinner. Sound good?"

"Where's Dad?"

"He moved his bowling night from Monday." Mom lifts an eyebrow and adds, pointedly, "Remember?"

"Oh, right." It's my parents' anniversary at the end of the week. Every year they fly up to Jackson for a few nights to eat at fancy restaurants and stay in a hotel and pretend they're young and carefree again. "I remember."

Mom pulls her hair loose from her hair tie and shakes it out around her shoulders as she starts up the stairs. "Oh, and you might want to ease up on those movies," she says. "I could hear you screaming all the way outside."

As soon as she's gone, I grab my phone off the floor and hurry down the hall to Dad's study. Most of his books are in the living room, but he keeps the R-rated stuff behind his desk.

I hesitate at the door, waiting until I hear the shower switch on upstairs. I slip inside, climbing onto Dad's desk chair so I can reach the higher shelves. I run my fingers over rows of beat-up spines, studying the titles.

The Devil's Hostage.

Banished from the Kingdom.

God Is Dead.

Exorcism and Deliverance.

I pull them down one by one and settle myself behind Dad's desk. My fingers shake as I turn the tissue-thin pages. The tiny type blurs before my eyes.

. . . valid possession can cause the most devastating insanity . . .

Satan has the authority to thwart God's will . . .

How to protect your soul from demonic interference . . .

. . . most documented possessions are preceded by vivid hallucinations and unshakable paranoia.

Nausea twists my stomach as I read. The books go on like that for pages. There are case files of real possessions. Stories from family members and neighbors. Doctors' reports. Pastor Joe said I was possessed, but he was crazy and sadistic. I didn't expect him to be right.

I turn a page—then flinch. A black-and-white photograph glares up at me. It shows a skeletally thin girl lying on a bed, her eyes and mouth open, blood smeared across her upper lip. She leers at the camera, nostrils flared. I study her eyes for a long moment. There's nothing behind those eyes. Nothing human, at least.

A caption beneath the photograph reads *Anna Harvey ten days before her death.*

Someone screams. It's a ragged, animal sound, and it rips through the silence in my house like teeth through skin. I sit straight up. For a moment, my fear is a living thing. It squeezes my chest. It breathes against the back of my neck, sending goose bumps down my spine.

The scream cuts off. The sudden quiet is almost as shocking. I hesitate, wondering if I'd imagined it. I listen for any other sound in the house. Floorboards creaking. The shower running. But there's only silence.

I stand, my eyes darting around the room for anything I could use as a weapon. Dad plays squash—there's a racquet in his closet. I hurry across the room and pull open the door. Dad's squash racquet is next to a pair of rain boots. I grab it with trembling hands.

"Hello?" I call.

Night has come, and shadows pool in the corners of the room. Wind howls outside, sending tree branches brushing against the windows. I creep out of the study, stepping into the hall.

"Mom?" I shout. "Was that you?"

Nothing. I move down the hall to the kitchen and flip the light. Nerves crawl up my arms and legs, but the kitchen is empty. I double-check the window with the broken lock to make sure the broom handle is holding. It's still firmly in place.

I move through the rest of the house, checking locks and peering through windows. I look behind furniture and inside of closets. I turn on every single light. No one.

Mom is still in the shower. I hear the sound of water beating against tile. I head upstairs. The wooden stairs feel rough beneath my bare feet. The air around me drops by several degrees, making me shiver. I hold Dad's racquet out in front of me, my heart beating so wildly that I can't hear anything else.

One step. Two. Wood creaks beneath my feet. Sweat gathers between my hands and the racquet's rubbery handle. I step off the stairs and onto the carpeted floor.

My parents' bedroom is down the hall. It's dark, the only light coming from the cracks around the bathroom door. I peer into the shadows, half expecting a face to separate from the darkness. The sound of the shower is louder in here. I tighten my grip on the racquet.

"Mom? Are you okay?" I call. I make out the shape of her kneepads on the floor, next to a pile of discarded clothes. There's a towel hanging from the bathroom door. The door is open a crack, and I can see the edge of the bath mat. The corner of the tub.

Something flickers at the corner of my eye. I whirl around, swinging the racquet, my heart hammering. But there's nothing there.

The shower switches off.

"Brooklyn?" my mom calls. "Is that you out there?"

I sink to the floor, dropping the racquet. "Yeah," I choke out. "It's me."

I lower my head to my hands and release a sob. My shoulders shake, and for a long time I can't catch my breath.

I'm going crazy. Absolutely, batshit crazy. I never should have gone to the pastor's house that night. I never should have let him die. I'm being punished. Tears trail down my cheeks. I can't do this anymore. It's got to stop.

I close my eyes, waiting for my heart rate to go back to normal.

Most documented possessions are preceded by vivid hallucinations and unshakable paranoia, I think.

I nick an Ambien from Dad's medicine cabinet after dinner and crawl into bed. It's not quite ten yet—way too early for sleep—but I don't care. I tell my parents that I feel sick. This day needs to be over. I pull my comforter all the way up to my nose. A car drives past my window, headlights arcing over my wall. I count the cracks in the ceiling until my eyes start to droop. . . .

A minute later sunshine is drifting through the thin curtains covering my window.

I yawn. I actually slept. It's a miracle. My eyes feel heavy, with goop gathered in the corners. I rub it away and sit up, stretching my arms over my head.

A full night of sleep has put everything into perspective. The scream was part of a nightmare. There was never anyone here. I'm just freaked because of everything that happened with Pastor Joe, but I'm not actually possessed. That's ludicrous.

I crawl out of bed, pulling the curtains away from my window to let in the sunlight. There's something on the other side of the glass. My eyes are still bleary, and it takes me a second to focus. My chest clenches.

There's a single dead rose taped outside of my window, its petals black and withered.

CHAPTER NINETEEN

I race outside, still in my pajamas. It's a hallucination, I tell myself. Just like the body parts in the tub, and the scream from last night. It's post-traumatic stress. None of it is real.

I throw open the front door and hurry down the steps, ducking beneath the gnarly oaks in our yard. The rose is still taped to the glass. Its withered stem bends under the weight of the dying flower head. Black petals litter the windowsill.

I approach slowly, like it's a bomb about to go off. Dewy grass dampens the bottoms of my feet. Wind rustles the tree branches and chills the skin on my bare arms. I peel the tape away, and the rose falls apart in my hand. Petals drift to the ground, tickling my toes.

It's not a hallucination. This flower is very, *very* real.

I jerk my head up, half convinced I'll see someone lurking in the shadows. But there's no one here. There's no sign of who left the rose for me at all.

I back away from the clearing and then turn and race up the stairs. Once inside, I lock the dead bolt and peek out the tiny window in the door to make sure there's no one there.

I inhale, and the smell of smoke fills my nostrils. I creep down the hallway toward the kitchen. The smell is stronger in here. It reminds me of that time we tried to use the fireplace without opening the flue. And the air seems thick—almost hazy. Something's burning.

I try to remember if I used the stove for any reason last night. Did I light a burner for tea and forget to turn it off? Did I switch the oven on for some reason or put something metal in the microwave? But I can't remember anything. I pull my pajama shirt over my nose, blinking against the smoke. I make my way to the oven, but it's not on. The burners are cold.

"Mom? Dad?" I shout. "Are you guys awake?"

No one answers. The smoke grows thicker. My eyes start to water. I haven't been able to light a candle since that night in Pastor Joe's bathroom, and it's too warm for the fireplace.

I wander through the living room and bathroom, searching for the source of the smoke. I check out my parents' bedroom, but they're both still asleep, their bodies two lumps beneath their thick duvet. I pull their door closed. The smoke seems to be coming from the air itself.

I'm starting to feel dizzy. The smoke clings to my nostrils. It coats the inside of my throat. I open a window in the living room, but that doesn't help. If anything, the smoke seems thicker.

"*Brooklyn . . . ,*" someone calls.

I freeze. I know that voice.

"*Brooklyn? Are you still out there?*"

I turn in place. It's coming from inside the bathroom. Pastor Joe releases a deep, phlegmy cough. Just like he did that night, when I left him inside his own bathroom to die.

You aren't here, I think, taking a step toward the bathroom door.

"*Please. The candle . . .*"

"You aren't here!" I shout. Smoke gets into my mouth, and I double over, coughing.

"*Can't put out the fire . . . ,*" Pastor Joe says, choking.

I reach for the doorknob. *This is all in my head*, I think, twisting. It's all in my—

I whip the door open quickly, like pulling off a Band-Aid.

The bathroom is empty. No candles. No dead pastor. No ghosts. I collapse against the wall, relief flooding through me. He's not here. He's dead. I inhale, and that's when I realize—the smoke is gone, too. The air is clear again.

The next day, I stand at the far corner of the sidewalk, staring at the stream of people walking through Christ First's main doors. The church's pale brick walls look dusty in the early morning sunshine. The golden cross gleams over the entrance.

It's Pastor Joe's funeral. I'm not going to stay for the whole thing, but I need to see his body in a coffin. I need to stare down at his pale, motionless face and know for sure that he's dead. That's the only way to make these hallucinations stop.

I put one foot in front of the other, slowly making my way closer to the church. I've never been to a funeral before. It feels like everyone is staring at me. A girl I've never met leans over to whisper something in her neighbor's ear. Another girl looks away as I walk past, like she can't stand to see my face. I know it's my imagination. These people can't possibly know what I did. But it feels real.

A boy coughs, loudly, and I swear I hear the word *murderer*. I whirl around.

"Did you say something?" I ask him. He looks at me, confused.

"What—"

"Brooklyn!" someone shouts, interrupting him. I turn as a girl moves away from a small group of mourners and races toward me. "Oh my god, is that you?"

"Hope?" I go stiff as Hope throws her arms around my shoulders, half afraid that she's just another hallucination.

Hope lets go of me and takes a step back. "Wow, your hair," she says, touching a blond strand. "It looks great. When did you bleach it?"

I'm still so surprised to see her. It takes me a moment to find my voice.

"Um, yesterday." I lean closer. "Are you okay? Where have you been? I've been texting you!"

"I know. Gavin and I have been staying with our aunt in Hope Springs."

Hope drops my hair and stares down at her hands. "It keeps hitting me at weird moments. It's all gone. *He's* gone."

I knot my hands together so tightly that the blood drains from the tips of my fingers. *He's gone because of me,* I think. *Because I didn't help him.*

I'm still trying to think of something comforting to say to Hope, but she looks up, brushing her long, black hair over one shoulder. She takes me by the arm and moves me away from the rest of the crowd.

"I know I should be in mourning," she whispers. "But I'm not. I've never been happier."

I stare at her for a moment, sure I didn't hear that right. "What?"

"I'm a terrible person," she says, her cheeks reddening. "I know I shouldn't admit it aloud. But I'm the happiest I've ever been in my life. Since he's been gone, it's like the sun has come out from behind a cloud. I don't have to worry about being punished anymore. I don't have to analyze everything I say or everything I do, just in case he decides that it's wrong. I finally feel free."

A tear slides down Hope's cheek, but she makes no move to brush it away. "I feel like I have you to thank for that," she says.

My throat feels suddenly dry. She can't know. There's no way she could possibly know.

"Why?" I choke out, swallowing.

"Remember the party you took me to? How you got me to admit to everything that's been happening?" Hope bites her bottom lip. "That was the first time I really thought about what my father and Gavin were doing to me. I thought you'd think there was something wrong with me, that you'd judge me for what was happening. But you didn't. You seemed really freaked out, like he was doing something wrong. I can't explain it, but I think that's the reason he's gone. I just wanted to tell you thank you for that. And for everything else. For being a friend."

Hope gives me a small, innocent smile. I nod, doing my best to look like I agree with her. But I know the truth. I know what really killed Pastor Joe.

"Hope I—" I start, but I can't quite bring myself to admit what happened that night. And why should I? Hope is safe. So why do I still feel guilty?

I swallow and try again. "I'm glad that you're okay."

"Me too," Hope says. This time, when she hugs me, I hug her back.

She feels small and frail in my arms. So easy to hurt. *I did the right thing,* I think.

She takes a step back, anxiously straightening her simple black dress. "Ready to go inside?"

I take Hope's hand and squeeze. "Let's do it."

Pastor Joe's service is in the main chapel, an auditorium-sized room that looks like it seats five thousand people. Every single pew is filled to max capacity, and there are people wandering up and down the aisles, looking for a seat. I look from face to face. I wonder, bitterly, whether they'd still be here if they saw the cuts across my back. My skin flares, reminding me.

"Come on," Hope says. "Family sits up front."

I follow her to the front of the auditorium. White lilies line the steps leading to the stage and crowd around the back wall. Their scent hangs heavy in the air, sweet and cloying.

I take my seat, grateful not to see Gavin on the bench. Someone heads up the steps to the pulpit, the wood creaking beneath his feet.

The microphone releases a hiss of static. "Thank you all for coming."

Nerves crawl up my spine. Gavin leans over the microphone, wearing a black suit with a white rose in the lapel. There might be five thousand people crowded in this chapel, but Gavin stares directly at me.

I wish I could sink into the floor. I wish lightning would rip through the ceiling and kill me on the spot. But since neither of those two things are likely, I stare right back at my ex-boyfriend, doing my best to look like he doesn't bother me. I cross my arms over my chest and tilt my head, daring him to make a scene.

A small, private smile curls Gavin's lips. "Pastor Joe wasn't just my father. He was my mentor, too," he says, his magnified voice booming off the chapel walls. "He taught me everything I know about God. And love. The church asked me to read something in honor of him. I chose a passage he respected greatly, one he referenced many times."

Gavin opens the Bible on the stand in front of him and clears his throat. *"Love is patient. Love is kind. . . ."*

His eyes never leave my face. It's like he's saying it directly to me. I shift in my seat, suddenly uncomfortable.

"It does not envy. It does not boast. . . ."

Heat rises in my cheeks. Gavin turns a page in the Bible too violently, and it rips from the spine. He lets it flutter to the ground, still not looking away from me. People start to whisper.

"It does not dishonor others," he says, and now his words sound angry. Pointed. *"It is not self-seeking, it is not easily angered. . . ."*

His eyes burn. I can't take it anymore. Shooting Hope an apologetic look, I lean to the person next to me and whisper, "Excuse me." He reluctantly moves his legs. I slip down the aisle.

"Love does not delight in evil!" Gavin shouts, his voice ringing through the crowded chapel. I keep my head ducked as I hurry toward the main doors. I hear people turning in their seats, watching me race out of the room. I lift my head, and—

Pastor Joe stands in front of the chapel doors wearing his usual polo and faded jeans, a baseball cap pulled low over his face. He tilts his head up and stares out from under the brim with his one remaining eye.

His face is burned and blackened. Skin drips from his chin and nose, like candle wax. It gathers in thick, knotty whorls around his eye sockets and over his cheeks and jaw. Bits of bone peek through the shredded tissue, white beneath the red and black. His ruined eye socket is a hollow mess of meat and blood and skin. A slithering, white maggot pokes its head through the gore and falls, trembling, to the ground.

Pastor Joe's gnarled lips spread into a wide smile, revealing a row of broken teeth and bloody gums. He winks at me with his good eye.

I open my mouth and scream.

CHAPTER TWENTY

My scream echoes off the surrounding walls, ringing through the chapel like a bell. It seems to hang in the air even after I close my mouth. Everyone falls silent, watching me. Nobody seems to notice the dead pastor standing in front of the doors.

No, I think. I grab my head with both hands, like I might be able to pull the hallucination out of my brain with my fingers. This can't be happening again. Not here. I squeeze my eyes shut and, when I open them again, I see—

No one. There's no one in front of the doors.

Whispers erupt in the crowd. They're all looking at me. Talking about me. I spot Riley sitting near the aisle, a smirk on her face, like she'd predicted this would happen. Tomorrow everyone will have heard this story. Not just the people at Christ First, but everyone at school. Everyone in Friend. They'll all think I'm a lunatic.

Hope stands, her face creased with concern. She tries to push her way out of her pew. "Brooklyn—"

She shouldn't have to deal with me now. Not during her father's funeral. I race out of the chapel and down the hall, tearing through the first set of doors I see—it's the bathroom, thank God. The same one where Gavin first bandaged my leg—and where I met Hope. The door swings shut behind me, and I lean against the wood, closing my eyes. A faucet drips, the sound hollow and haunting.

Pastor Joe's face is burned on the inside of my lids. Bloody tissue oozes out of his ruined mouth. Burnt flesh hangs from his nose and chin.

My eyes fly open again. My heart thuds in my ears, and I can't seem to catch my breath.

He's haunting me. I let him die and now he's punishing me for it.

I lurch toward the sinks and switch on the faucet. Cold, clear water comes pouring out. I dip my hands under the water and splash my face, trying to steady my breathing.

"It's going to be okay," I say to the empty room. I force myself to inhale, sucking in breath until I can't fill my lungs any further. And then I exhale, slowly, pretending I'm a balloon leaking air. My heartbeat calms. Nerves stop scratching at my skin. "It's all going to be—"

The faucet sputters. I flinch, nerves humming back to life. It spits.

The water turns cloudy, and a foul smell fills the air. I move away from the sink, trembling. I *know* that smell. It's just like the rancid holy water Pastor Joe poured over my face in his bathroom.

My legs start to tremble. I prop an arm against the wall to hold myself up.

"It's all in your head," I whisper. "It's all in your—"

Another faucet spurts on. And another, until there's water streaming out of all four sinks lining the opposite wall. Steam rises up from them. The smell is putrid— like rotten eggs and sewage and old fish. It fills the entire room. I back toward the door, choking on the stench. I fumble for the doorknob, but I can't turn it. It's locked.

Water dribbles over the edge of the sink and onto the tile. The smell is so thick. I can't breathe. I try the door again, and this time the knob twists. I stumble into the hallway.

Gavin is waiting outside the bathroom door. He straightens when he sees me. "Brooklyn?"

"Gavin." I jerk to a stop. I clench my hands together to keep them from trembling and force myself to say, "I . . . I'm really sorry for your loss."

"Thanks." Gavin's voice is hollow. His hair looks unwashed, and the skin around his eyes is red and swollen. He leans forward, like he's about to hug me, and I jerk backward. I can't look at him without seeing the bruises on Hope's back, or hearing the hitch in her voice when she confessed what Gavin and his father did to her.

A hundred different emotions fight across his face, but the strongest one seems to be hurt. His eyes move to my hair. "You're blond," he says. "I like it."

"Thanks." I try to move past him and start down the hallway.

He grabs me by the arm. "Wait. I want to talk to you."

"I should really go."

His fingers pinch my skin. "Two minutes."

"Please let go of me." I jerk my arm away a little too violently, and Gavin stumbles back a step, his eyes widening. I glance back at him, an apology on my lips, but I catch sight of the swinging bathroom door before I can speak. It flies open, and I see a row of empty sinks. A dry floor. It swings shut again.

The hallucination—or whatever the hell it was—is over. I press a hand to my chest, letting my breathing deepen. Gavin is talking, but I haven't heard a word that's come out of his mouth.

"What did you say?" I ask.

He blinks. "I just . . . I was saying that I overreacted the other day," he repeats in a softer voice. "And that I'm sorry."

"You're sorry?" My voice sounds hollow.

Gavin smiles, sadly. "I was hoping we could go some-place. Maybe talk for a while?"

He takes my hand in his, weaving his fingers through mine.

I look down at our entwined fingers. He keeps grabbing and pulling at me, like he thinks my body is something he can control.

I tug my hand free from his. "I don't think that's a good idea."

The corners of his eyes crinkle. "You don't mean that."

"I'm sorry."

I try to walk away, but Gavin pushes past me, prop-ping an arm against the wall to block the hallway. There's a tight, angry look to his face that I've never seen before. His nostrils flare.

I stop walking and cross my arms over my chest. "Let me go."

"You shouldn't trust her," he snaps. "This is what she does. She's just going to fuck with your head."

I take a step back, throwing my hands up to show that I'm done with this conversation. I'm done with *him*.

"Stay away from me," I say, turning around. There are other ways out of this building.

I've never been so excited for a school day before. Normally, the thought of another Monday surrounded by superficial phonies and idiot teachers would give me an instant migraine. Today, I practically skip down the sidewalk.

"Are the rumors true?"

I turn. Riley stands at the corner, flanked by Grace and Alexis. They look like a three-person cult.

"What are you talking about?" I ask.

Riley's lips quirk. It's her signature "I know something you don't know" evil bitch smile. It curves her lips for a fraction of a second and then vanishes completely.

"You changed your hair," she says. "It looks . . . great." She studies my spiky blond pixie cut, clearly unimpressed.

I resist the urge to roll my eyes. "Riley?" I try again. "What rumors?"

She looks from Grace to Alexis, both of whom are wearing the exact same fake sad expression. I wonder if they planned it beforehand. Like how girlfriends plan to wear the same outfits when they're little. I wonder if Alexis and Grace had to practice in the mirror for hours to get that pouty lip thing right.

"Just that you broke Gavin's heart," Riley says.

"Is that right?" I ask.

"That's what everyone's saying. Apparently he's *destroyed*."

Something about how she says this sends nerves dancing around in my stomach. It's the way she emphasizes the word *destroyed*. It twists inside her mouth. Sounding wrong.

"His dad just died, Riley. That's why he's destroyed," I say. But Riley doesn't seem to hear me. Or care. She strolls up the sidewalk, her heels scraping at the concrete. Her eyes are sharp and narrow. Like they might cut me.

"You should be more careful," Alexis says, as the three of them walk past me. "It's pretty easy to get a reputation in this town."

"Be a shame for people to think the wrong thing," Grace adds.

They walk away without saying another word. I watch their retreating figures disappear into the school, feeling like I've been slapped.

I have a few minutes to kill before history class, so I head to the library and slam my backpack onto a table in the far corner, right next to the row of windows overlooking the football field. A few stoners huddle beneath the bleachers, passing a joint from hand to hand.

Our library is shit. Every book is at least twenty years old, and people only ever use the row of shiny, brand-new computers up front, anyway. The librarian is bent over a student right now, studying something on one of the screens. I could skin a cat back here and she wouldn't look up until it started to smell.

I drop into a chair. The word *reputation* rings in my ears. I didn't realize girls still used that word as code for *slut*. It's such a cliché.

I pull my trusty Sharpie from my backpack. Uncap it.

Riley Howard is a whore, I scrawl across the tabletop. The words give me a sick sort of rush. I dig my teeth into my lips as I dot all the *i*'s with tiny black hearts.

I should just leave it here. She deserves it. But I scribble the words out anyway, digging the tip of my Sharpie deep into the wood on the table. Riley might be a bitch now, but we were friends once. I'm not going to stoop to her level.

I stretch my legs under the table, curling my toes into my combat boots. I tap the Sharpie against the side of my backpack. A car drives past the school, and the sudden roar of the engine makes me flinch. I watch it disappear down the street, and only then do I notice that the stoners are gone. The space beneath the bleachers is empty except for a few roaches and . . . something.

I frown and lean forward in my chair. The foreign object beneath the bleachers seems ominous somehow. It's long and thin and dark, and it definitely doesn't belong on the beer-stained pavement. I don't know why I even care, but I find myself pushing my chair back and crossing over to the window. Shielding my eyes as I peer through the glass.

Recognition vibrates through my skin a second before my eyesight clears. Black petals. A long, thorny stem. It's a fucking *rose*. A dead rose, just like the one someone taped to my bedroom window.

I reel away from the windows like I've been stung, tripping over my chair. I slam into the floor butt-first, and a few of the kids snicker into closed fists. Someone claps, but the librarian snaps something at him.

All of this happens in the background. I barely register it because I'm still staring at that damn rose, and my heart is vibrating so fast I can't count individual beats anymore.

Gavin left me that rose. I'm sure of it like I've never been sure of anything before. And if he left me that one, it means he left the one outside my bedroom, too. It means he's been watching me. Following me.

I stand, pulling the chair upright as I scan the football field. There's no one. Wind ripples over the grass. A bird crosses the sky, its shadow flickering over the ground below. When I'm sure that Gavin's not about to pop out from behind a tree, I pull my phone out of my backpack.

Wilderness. Lunchtime, I text Deirdre. **Something fucked up is going on.**

Deirdre is already sprawled across the puke-yellow couch in The Wilderness when I duck out during lunch, one leg thrown over a ratty cushion, her curly head leaning against the arm. I push through the trees, and she lifts her eyes without moving her head.

"Check this out," she says, propping herself up on one arm. "See that cloud there?"

I plop onto the couch next to her and crane my neck back. "There?"

"Yeah. Doesn't that look like a penis?"

I smack her on the shoulder, and she collapses back against the couch, giggling. "Perv."

"I'm serious! See those two really round clouds right at the . . . er . . . base?"

I roll my eyes, but I follow Deirdre's pointing finger, and she's right. The cloud does sort of look like a penis.

I groan and kick my feet up onto the couch. A thick plume of dust escapes from the cushions and settles on our outstretched legs. Except for us, The Wilderness is deserted. Which is weird. Adams High lets us eat lunch outside, and there are usually a couple of kids who bring their food out here to avoid sitting on the bleachers with all the cheerleaders and asshole jocks.

"Where is everyone?" I ask. Deirdre shrugs.

"It was empty when I got here. So. Something fucked up is going on."

"What?"

"That's what you texted. 'Something fucked up is going on.' Remember?"

"Oh. Right." I close my eyes, pushing down against the lids with my thumb and forefinger. This morning the only thing I wanted to do was bitch to Deirdre about how creepy Gavin was being.

I open my eyes. "It's Gavin. He got weird."

"Weird how?"

I tell her about the roses Gavin left for me, knowing full well she won't be able to deal with the whole truth.

Deirdre frowns when I finish my story. "You dumped him right after his dad died?"

I chew my lower lip. I can't explain why I did that without explaining about Hope and the torture and everything else. Suddenly I can't think of anything I want to talk about less. I lean back against the couch cushions and stare up at the sky. The wind has blown the penis cloud apart. Now it doesn't look like anything.

"See that one?" I ask, pointing. "It looks sort of like a . . ."

Something moves in the trees to my left. I drop my arm and push myself up again, frowning. There's nothing there.

"Hey." Deirdre sits up and waves a hand in front of my face. "What's up?"

"Nothing," I say, my eyes still trained on the spot between the trees. My brain hums, trying to figure out what I thought I saw, but the picture is fuzzy. It was a shadow. Something that wasn't supposed to be there.

I feel that humming sensation just below my skin. Like there's electricity thrumming through my veins and bones. Deirdre says something, but I don't hear her. I push myself to my feet and take a step toward the trees. I don't even bother telling myself that it was just a squirrel or a bird. I know what it was. Who it was.

The grass between the trees is all flattened, like someone had just been standing here. I look around for Gavin, but he's already gone.

"Brooklyn?" Deirdre pushes herself off the couch, a note of concern in her usually carefree voice. "What the hell?"

I shove my hands into my pockets, trying to shake the loose, nervy feeling creeping through my bones. "It's nothing—"

I stop talking, my eyes catching on something on the tree in front of me. Deirdre comes up behind me, her eyes widening as she sees what I'm staring at.

Someone's carved a shape into the bark. A jerky heart, the edges rough and splintery.

"Holy shit," Deirdre murmurs, covering her mouth with her hand. "Did he do that?"

I nod, running a finger over the shape. A tiny splinter of wood pricks my skin, drawing blood.

CHAPTER TWENTY-ONE

"How are the potatoes?" Dad asks, scraping his fork against his plate. "Too salty?"

I stab a potato with my fork. "Yum," I say, sticking it in my mouth. They *are* too salty, but I swallow anyway. Dad can be sensitive about his cooking.

My iPhone buzzes next to my plate. I glance at the screen—it's a text from Hope.

"No phone at the dinner table," Dad says. "You know the rule."

"Yeah, sorry." I flip my cell over, so I can't see the screen, and turn my attention back to the food. Dad went all out tonight: steak, potatoes, and asparagus wrapped in prosciutto. They're catching a plane right after dinner, and Dad hates airport food.

I stab a spear of asparagus with my fork and lift it to my mouth. My eyes travel back over to my cell phone. I can practically hear Hope's text calling to me.

The kitchen door swings open and Mom bustles in.

"Sorry, I know I'm late," she says, as the door slams shut behind her. Her oversized Coach purse hangs from one arm, along with a blue mesh lunch box and a tote bag. She has two more tote bags looped around the other arm, and she's holding a brown paper sack. "Did you save me some?"

"There's a plate for you in the fridge," Dad says, shoveling another forkful of mashed potatoes into his mouth. "But we need to leave in five minutes if we're going to make the flight."

"I'll eat fast." Mom drops the rest of her bags on the floor and hurries into the kitchen. She returns a moment later with a plate balanced on one hand, Saran wrap peeled back as she picks at the food with her fingers. "Are we all packed?"

While they talk carry-ons and luggage fees, I flip my phone over and tap a finger against the screen. Hope's cheerful text bubble blinks up at me. **You around this weekend? Want to stop by band practice?**

I think of black flower petals scattered beneath the bleachers. A jerky heart carved into a tree. The thought of ever being in the same room with Gavin again makes my skin feel two sizes too small.

Can't, I type back. I hit send and move the phone back under my plate.

Mom slides into the chair next to me.

"How was your day? You feeling better?" she asks, putting the back of her hand to my forehead.

"Fine." I flinch back from her touch. "I feel fine."

My iPhone buzzes again, and I flip it over without thinking. Another text.

Did I do something wrong?

Mom glances over my shoulder before I can flip the phone over. "Hope?" she asks. "We haven't met her, have we?"

"Not yet." I stab the steak with my fork, but instead of bringing it to my mouth I dunk it in my mashed potatoes and swirl it around. "So what's the deal? You guys aren't back until Wednesday, right? Because I was thinking Deirdre could stay over."

My parents don't love Deirdre, but there's no way I'm sleeping here alone with my stalker ex leaving gifts taped to my window. Mom exchanges a look with Dad, and he puts his fork down, folding his hands.

"Your mom and I were thinking, kiddo," he says. The word *kiddo* makes me cringe. "We're not sure you should be left alone right now."

"You've seemed stressed," Mom adds.

"You guys aren't staying home because of me, are you?" I scrape my fork over my plate, causing a high-pitched shriek that makes my mother cringe. "Because that's crazy. I'm fine."

Mom and Dad exchange another look. "Actually—"

My phone rings. My phone never rings, and the sound is so foreign to me that I actually flinch and look around before I realize where it's coming from.

Mom clears her throat. "You know that thing is supposed to be off."

"Sorry." I glance at the screen. Hope again. My fingers itch to pick up the phone, but I curl them toward my palms, letting it go to voice mail instead. "Um, what were you saying?"

"We thought you might not want to spend the whole night alone, so I asked Elijah to stop by and check in," Dad finishes. "You and Elijah get along, right?"

I blink. "What?"

"He should be here soon," Mom adds, leaning over Dad's lap to check his watch. "We told him anytime after eight would be good."

Two conflicting emotions go to war inside of my chest. On the one hand, it sounds like Dad just called the boy I like to come *watch* me while they were out of town. Like a *babysitter*.

On the other hand, Elijah is coming over. And my parents won't be here. I think of our kiss from a few nights ago, and warmth spreads through my chest. I can practically feel his hair between my fingers, his lips pressed to mine.

My phone rings. I glance at the screen—Hope again.

"I really should get this," I say, picking it up. "She thinks I'm mad at her, and . . ."

Dad waves the rest of my explanation away. "It's fine. We need to get moving, anyway."

He taps his watch with one finger and motions for Mom to hurry it up. She half-stands, shoving one last baby potato into her mouth.

"You'll get the dishes?" she asks, pressing a napkin to her lips.

"Yeah, sure," I say. I lift the phone to my ear, stepping into the hallway so Hope and I can talk in private. "Hey," I say, easing the door closed behind me. "Everything cool?"

"That's what I was going to ask you." She sounds nervous. "Your text was vague. Did I do something?"

"No! We're fine."

"Then why are you being weird?"

I lean my head back against the wall, sighing. "Look, I didn't want to put you in the middle of this, but Gavin has been a little . . . intense since we broke up. I don't really want to see him right now."

Hope is silent for a beat. "Intense how?"

I swallow, thinking of black roses and jagged hearts carved into tree bark. "He's been following me around. Leaving stuff for me, that sort of thing. I'm handling it, but showing up at band practice might give him the wrong message."

"That's pretty screwed up," Hope says. "I can talk to him—"

"No, don't—"

The door creaks open, and my mom pokes her head into the hall. I tell Hope to hold on a second and lower the phone from my ear. "Are you guys leaving?"

Mom nods. "There's cash on the table for pizza."

"And plenty of leftovers in the fridge!" Dad calls from the other room. "Don't order out every night."

A second later, I hear the front door slam shut.

"Are you still there?" I ask, lifting my phone back to my ear.

"Yeah," Hope says. "So Gavin is, like, stalking you? Is that what you're saying?"

Stalking. Up until now, I haven't let myself say that word out loud. But he's following me around. Watching me sleep. Leaving weird things for me to find. Spreading rumors about me.

I swallow. "I don't know what I'd call it. I think I should give him some space."

The doorbell rings. My "babysitter" must be here.

"I should go," I tell Hope, starting down the hall to the front door. "Thanks for listening. I appreciate it."

"Any time. You know I'm here for you, right?"

"Yeah. Thanks."

I hang up the phone and pull the front door open. Elijah is kneeling on the porch.

"Oh! Hey, I was just about to ring the bell again," he says, standing.

"And instead you decided to say a quick prayer to our doormat?"

"Ha ha." Elijah looks up at me, and his eyes widen. "Whoa," he says. "You changed your hair."

"Oh yeah." I touch a strand, self-consciously. "You like it?"

"It's . . . blond."

"That's the point. Come on in," I say, stepping aside to let Elijah through the front door.

He hands me a small glass bottle. "Any idea where this came from?"

I frown, taking the bottle from Elijah's fingers. It's filled with some sort of dark liquid. I turn it around, watching the liquid coat the sides of the glass. It's thick, and so dark it's almost black. I hold it up to the sun and see that it has a slightly reddish tint to it.

"This is so weird," I say. "It almost looks like—"

Understanding hits me like a punch to the gut. The

bottle slips from my fingers and hits the floor with a sharp crack. I scream and leap backward, but, luckily, the glass doesn't break.

Elijah frowns at me. "Brooklyn? What is it?"

"Blood," I say, still staring at the tiny bottle. "Gavin left me a bottle of his blood."

CHAPTER TWENTY-TWO

E lijah won't stop moving.

"How long has this been going on?" he asks, pacing the length of the living room. He's all manic energy, his limbs jittering and shaking. My parents' books tremble on their shelves with each of his angry footsteps.

I perch at the edge of the couch, curling my hands in my lap. Unlike Elijah, I don't want to move. I want to stay very still and make myself small, and then, maybe, I'll disappear and no one can leave vials of their own blood on my front porch anymore.

"Just since his dad died," I choke out. I pull my knees to my chest and knot my arms around them. "He got weird when I broke up with him, and I think that and the grief—"

Elijah stops walking. "So you did break up with him?"

I nod. Elijah looks like he might say something else, but instead, he turns around, propping both hands on his hips. He's not pacing anymore, but he doesn't exactly seem still, either. His body looks like it's made of jagged lines. Like he might explode.

"We need to call your parents," he says, after a moment. "They won't want you staying here alone with some . . . stalker roaming around."

"They'll be back in a few days."

"They should come back *now*," Elijah shouts. I flinch, even though I know his anger isn't about me. I've never seen him so mad before. He's usually calm and laid-back, like everything is a big joke. This is unnerving.

I roll my lower lip between my teeth and stare down at the floor. There's a crack in the wood, the edges all splintery.

The only way to get my parents to turn around from the airport would be to tell them *everything*. That I disobeyed them and went to look for my mystery caller. That I met a boy at a cultish church. That we started dating—and I sort of forgot to tell them. That he turned out to be a slut-shaming, incestuous psycho.

They're going to start freaking out before we even get to the stalking part.

Elijah reads the hesitation on my face. "They don't know about Gavin, do they?"

"I was going to tell them," I mutter.

"Right." Elijah plops onto the couch next to me, his knees bouncing. He drops his head into his hands. "You can't stay here alone. You barely even know this Gavin guy. If he's going to leave a vial of blood on your porch, there's no telling what else he might do."

"He wouldn't hurt me," I say.

Elijah raises an eyebrow. "You know that for sure?"

I open my mouth and then close it again. Gavin knew what his father was doing to Hope, and he didn't do anything about it.

"No," I say, finally. "I don't."

Elijah leans back against the couch, his face tilted toward the ceiling. "I'm going to stick around. If that asshole comes back he's going to get a pretty nasty surprise."

Elijah spends the rest of the evening working on an essay in my dad's office while I try, again—and fail, again—to catch up on my reading for history. Before I get ready for bed we search the yard and porch to make sure Gavin hasn't left me any more delightful little "gifts."

"Nothing," Elijah says, checking under a bush near the stairs to the front porch. He sounds almost disappointed.

"You must've scared him off," I say.

"Must've," Elijah says, but he doesn't sound convinced. We head back up the stairs and into the house. I shut the front door behind me, checking the lock twice to make sure the dead bolt slides firmly into place.

Elijah's sitting on the couch when I return to the living room. He's got his head propped in his hands, his fingers burying into his hair. He looks up when I walk in.

"I really don't think it's a good idea for you to spend the night alone," he says.

"Oh?" I try to keep my voice nonchalant, but I'm not sure I manage. I've been dreading the thought of being alone in this house again. I've had to stop myself from counting the hours until Elijah leaves.

"You said he watched you sleep last night. And that's when he left the flowers and the blood. I think I should stay." Elijah clears his throat, his cheeks turning slightly pink. "On the couch, of course."

The corner of my mouth itches, and it's all I can do not to let the big goofy grin unfold across my face. Gavin won't pull anything with Elijah here.

"I'll get the spare sheets," I say, hopping off the couch.

"Kung Fu Panda?" Elijah asks when I return with the extra pillows and sheets. I start tucking the corners into the folds of the couch.

"I'll have you know that Kung Fu Panda was very big when I was seven years old."

Elijah grins and shoves a pillow into a brightly colored cartoon case. "If it was good enough for seven-year-old Brooklyn, I guess it's good enough for me."

I duck my head so he won't see me grin. I wonder if he sleeps in his boxers. I wonder if he snores.

"I should head to bed," I say, tossing the rest of the sheets onto the couch. "Sleep tight."

Elijah smiles. "You too."

My skin tingles. Yeah, right. Between the hot boy on my couch and the creepy boy hanging around outside my window, it'll be a miracle if I sleep at all tonight.

I need to figure out a way to relax, so I grab a towel and hurry into the bathroom down the hall. The tile feels cold beneath my feet, making me shiver. I turn on the faucet, twisting the knob to the hottest possible setting. Steam fills the small room. The air becomes thick and soupy. Condensation gathers on the mirror, slowly turning my reflection blurry.

I undress, cringing as the fabric brushes against the healing cuts along my back and arms. They aren't bleeding anymore, and some of the darker bruises have already started to fade. Soon, I can put all this behind me.

I step into the shower and duck below the scalding hot water. I close my eyes, lifting my face to the stream. It soothes my tense muscles, making me feel mercifully loose and numb. I duck my head, letting water run through my hair and down my back. I tilt my chin up again and catch the water in my mouth.

It tastes thick. Metallic.

I open my eyes and all I see is red. Red steam. Red water. I jerk out from under the stream of red pouring out from the showerhead. *Rust*, I think. There must be something wrong with the pipes. But it doesn't smell like rust. The smell is heavy and familiar.

Blood, I realize. The shower is spurting blood.

Vomit rises in my chest. I grab for the shower curtain, but it's slick beneath my fingers. I try to pull it aside and lose my balance, falling hard to the bottom of the tub. Blood rains down on me, staining my skin red, filling the air with its horrible, cloying scent. Like old pennies. I grope, wildly, for the side of the tub. The blood feels hotter than it was a second ago. Too hot. I glance down and see that it's begun to boil. Bubbles form and pop between my feet. I scream, the sound echoing off the tile walls and floor around me.

I finally manage to push the shower curtain aside and crawl out of the tub. Blood clings to my arms and legs and feet. I leave thick red prints on the tile floor. I pull a towel off the hook on the wall and try to scrub the blood from my skin. But it doesn't matter how hard I rub, the red won't go away. I can't get it off my skin.

I scramble to my feet, wrapping the towel around my bloody body. Hands trembling, I switch on the faucet in the sink. A thick stream of blood pours into the porcelain bowl. I scream again—louder this time—as panic builds in my chest.

Footsteps thud up the stairs, and a second later the door swings open.

"What happened?" Elijah asks, his eyes wide. My screams have turned to sobs. I can't manage to speak. I jerk my hand toward the stream of blood quickly filling the sink.

But—it's not blood anymore. It's water again, bubbling as it slides down the drain. I look down at myself. Water drips from my elbows and the ends of my hair. It pools beneath my feet.

Elijah frowns. "Brooklyn—"

"No," I murmur. I cross the bathroom and rip the curtain open, certain that I'll see blood spurting out of the shower, gathering at the bottom of the tub in a bubbling boil.

Clouds of steam overcome me, making me cough. When it clears, I see plain water cascading into the bathtub, clear as can be.

CHAPTER TWENTY-THREE

I t takes me longer than it should to get dressed. Maybe that's because I'm still trembling. My fingers shake so badly I can barely button my jeans. I may not be covered in blood anymore, but I can still feel it clinging to my skin. It's heavy and sticky, too thick to be water. The smell is trapped inside my nose.

I close my eyes, shuddering, and pull open the bathroom door. Elijah waits for me in the hallway.

"Are you okay?" he asks.

I shake my head. "Get me out of here."

Elijah opens his mouth, looking like he might argue.

"*Please*," I say, before he gets the chance. "We can just

drive for a while. I just . . . I can't deal with this house anymore."

"Fine," Elijah says, pulling his car keys out of his pocket. "Where do you want to go?"

I exhale and close my eyes, feeling like a huge weight has been lifted from my shoulders. "Anywhere," I say. "Just as long as we keep moving."

It takes twenty minutes to drive down every street in Friend. We do it twice, and while we drive I tell Elijah about Pastor Joe's death and my hallucinations.

"But it's not real," he insists, turning down Henry Street again. "You're just freaking out because of what happened to Pastor Joe."

"Maybe," I say. I didn't tell Elijah about my part in the pastor's death, but I keep thinking about what I read in my dad's books. There are other reasons I could be feeling unhinged. Darker reasons.

"You want to drive around this town all night?" Elijah asks as we zoom past my parents' house for the third time. I smile, watching the house grow smaller and smaller in the rearview mirror. There's something about aimless driving that makes it seem like all your problems are put on pause. There's a part of me that never wants to get out of this car.

"We should have a destination," I say after a moment. We're driving down Maple now, toward the subdivision where Riley lives.

"Where do you want to go?" Elijah asks.

I stare out the window at all the mini mansions flying past. I never understood why Riley and her parents needed so much space for the three of them. And it's not just the big house, either. They have the lake house, too, and they're hardly ever there.

Riley and I snuck up to the lake house once. It was early in the summer before freshman year, back when we were still bestest friends who did everything together. She convinced her boyfriend's older brother to drive us up and found the hide-a-key under the rock near the front porch. We spent the whole day swimming and laying out in the sun. There was very little food there, but we dug frozen pizzas out of the fridge, and Riley found a case of some insanely expensive local artisan beer of her dad's. I could barely drink that beer, it was so bitter, but I remember feeling so grown up, sitting on the deck with Riley and the boys, drinking and laughing.

I smile just thinking about it. That was the last really good memory I have of Riley's friendship. Later that summer we started growing apart, arguing about stupid things and getting annoyed more easily. But that day at the lake house was perfect. I almost wish I could live it over again.

"I have an idea," I say to Elijah.

* * *

It's pitch black when we pull up to Riley's family house on Lake Whitney, much darker than it was in the city. Elijah stops the car and cuts the engine. His headlights flick off.

"Are you sure about this?" he asks, peering at the house. I'd forgotten how beautiful it was. All weathered gray wood and floor-to-ceiling windows, the shadowy outlines of sleek, modern furniture visible just inside.

I throw open my door and climb out of the car. "They never come up here. It's October. Someone should enjoy it."

I kneel next to the front door, finding the fake rock that Riley and I hid in the bushes back when we were nine. I turn it over, and sure enough there's the little hide-a-key cubby beneath. I dig out the spare key and fit it into the lock.

"Yeah," Elijah says, coming up behind me. "But you don't think it's kind of . . . wrong?"

I hesitate, my hand still on the doorknob. I think about how Riley looked at me after I screamed inside the chapel, and what she said to me at school. *Be careful not to get a reputation.*

I turn the key, and the door creaks open. Maybe I want to do something wrong.

I step into the dark house, fumbling against the wall for a light switch. I find it, and the lamps in the living room flicker on, illuminating oversized leather furniture, a sleek flat-screen television, and a fireplace made of smooth gray rocks. The massive windows look out onto the lake during the day, but right now there's nothing but flat, black darkness beyond them. They almost look like painted walls instead of glass.

"What do you think?" I ask, turning in place. Elijah moves around the room in awe, his eyes wide.

"So Riley and her parents are, like, rich?" he says.

"Pretty much."

"I'm starting to wonder if I chose the wrong hot teenager to hook up with," he says.

"Hey!" I grab a pillow off the couch and swat him with it. He laughs and dances away from me.

"Just joking," he says, taking the pillow out of my hands. He lets it drop onto the couch.

"Better be," I mutter.

Elijah doesn't say anything. He pulls me into his arms, his eyes never leaving my face. I take in his full height. He's almost a head taller than me. I have to stand on tiptoes to get my arms around his shoulders.

"I think I'm too short for you," I say.

The corner of Elijah's mouth twitches. "Impossible. You'll just have to grow."

"Or you'll have to shrink."

Elijah bends his knees, crouching down until we're

eye level. His nose brushes against mine. His lips are just inches away. "Better?"

I nod, staring at those lips. I will them closer, and, like he can read my thoughts, Elijah leans toward me. His lips are firm and soft, and the stubble on his cheeks scratches my skin. I weave my hands behind his neck, and, for a moment, I forget about every terrible thing that's happened since I left Pastor Joe behind in that burning bathroom. It doesn't matter anymore. Not with Elijah's arms around me.

Elijah grabs me by the waist, his lips never moving from mine. He lifts me, easily, and I wrap my legs around his back. It was cold when we first got here, since the heat probably isn't on, but it doesn't feel cold now. Elijah's skin burns the tips of my fingers. Sweat gathers on the small of my back.

Elijah leans me onto the soft leather, one hand fumbling with my jeans. I shrug off my sweater and start working on the buttons of his flannel.

"There are tiny skulls on your bra," he says.

"Shut up," I mutter, kissing him again. His chest is firm and warm beneath my hands. I pull his shirt off and drop it onto the ground.

Elijah pushes a strand of hair behind my ear and kisses me on the cheek. "Is this okay?"

I'm suddenly very aware of how alone we are. The two of us in this house in the middle of nowhere, surrounded by trees and lake and empty space. There's no one out here to bother us. To stop us.

I reach behind my back and unhook my bra with one hand. "Don't stop."

"Should we light a fire?" Elijah asks.

I smile against his chest, listening to the steady sound of his heart beating beneath his ribs. "Would that mean moving?"

"Oh, right. Stupid plan."

I inch closer, and Elijah wraps an arm around my back. We're tangled together on the couch, a massive faux-fur blanket draped over us. A fire sounds nice, but I honestly can't imagine being any happier than I am at this moment. My whole body is warm and relaxed, and the steady sound of Elijah's breathing is lulling me to sleep. I've never felt as safe as I do in this moment.

"Should I make us some grilled cheese?" Elijah asks.

"You're talking about moving again."

"Just for a few minutes. To gather supplies." Elijah sits up, wrapping the blanket around his waist.

"If you're getting supplies anyway, maybe a fire wouldn't be so—"

Something thuds against the glass in the windows, making us both flinch.

I sit up, and just like that, all the relaxation and safety I felt only a few moments ago has vanished.

Nerves prickle over my skin. I stare out the window, but nothing penetrates the perfect, oily blackness surrounding us.

Elijah lowers a hand to my shoulder. "Maybe it was a bird."

"Maybe," I say. But I can't help feeling exposed. To anyone standing outside, Riley's lake house would be like a spotlight. They could be watching us right now and we'd have no idea. I tug my sweater over my head and pull my jeans back up my hips. I cross the room, shielding my eyes as I lean toward the window.

There's a handprint on the glass. My heart starts beating faster. I try to remember if I touched it when we got here—if Elijah did. But my mind goes blank. I reach out to wipe the handprint away, but it won't budge. It's on the other side of the window.

"Oh God," I say, jerking away. Elijah's suddenly behind me. He puts both hands on my shoulders, whirling me around.

"What's the matter?" he asks. "Did you see something?"

I glance back at the handprint, wondering if it's just another one of my hallucinations, if it'll disappear the second I point it out to Elijah. But Elijah follows my gaze, and his eyes widen at the sight of the print. He runs a finger, lightly, over the glass.

"Do you think there's someone out there?" I ask. Elijah narrows his eyes and peers into the darkness beyond the window. I look, too, but it's bright in here, dark out there. All I see is light bouncing off the glass, and my own face reflected back at me.

Elijah grabs his shirt off the floor and slips it back on, buttoning it unevenly. "I'm going to go check things out," he says. "If there's someone out there, he couldn't have gotten far."

"I'm coming with you." I grab my combat boots from the floor and start pulling them on.

Elijah frowns. "I don't think that's a good idea."

"You're not going out there alone."

"It would be better if you waited here," he insists. "If something happens, you could call the cops."

"They have these things called cell phones now, genius. I can call the cops from right next to you."

Elijah sighs, pinching the bridge of his nose between two fingers. "Please stay here," he says in a quieter voice. "I don't want anything to happen to you."

I sit back on the couch, defeated. "Fine," I say. "You're taking your phone, right?"

"The one that died in the car and is charging in the kitchen?"

I groan and nod at my own cell phone, which is sitting on the coffee table. Elijah leans over and scoops it up, then plants a kiss on my forehead. "Fine."

"And if you aren't back in five minutes, I'm coming to find you."

He shakes his head and pulls the door open, his shirt still buttoned wrong and hanging unevenly over his jeans. A second later, I see my phone spark to life outside. He's using the flashlight feature to send a steady white beam of light bouncing through the trees.

I stand and flip the light switch. The lamps scattered around the living room all flicker off. I press my face to the glass, watching Elijah walk toward the woods, his back to the house, my phone flashlight cutting through the darkness. My heartbeat steadies. Now that I can see what's happening outside, it doesn't seem so spooky. Just rocks and trees and lake. Nothing—

A shadow steps in front of the window. I jerk backward, eyes widening, as Gavin presses his face to the glass.

He looks like he hasn't slept. His eyes have a hollow, sunken look to them, and his skin is gray. He stares at me for a long moment.

Slut, he mouths.

"No," I say. Gavin turns and runs toward the woods. I can still see the flashlight flickering through the trees. I bang a fist against the window, and the glass trembles beneath my hand.

"Elijah!" I scream, but he's too far away. He'll never hear me. "Elijah!"

CHAPTER TWENTY-FOUR

The door slams shut, leaving me alone in the dark.

No, not alone. Gavin is out here, too.

"Elijah!" I shout. "Gavin?"

Trees sway in the wind. A breeze sends ripples over the glassy lake. I glance back at the lake house. I turned the lights on again before I left so I'd be able to find my way back in the dark. Their golden glow gives me comfort.

I exhale, and my breath hangs in front of my face in an icy cloud. Elijah's old Honda sits at the end of the driveway, a newer Subaru that must belong to Gavin right behind it. I look at the still, black woods and then at the cars again. Something sour hits the back of my throat.

Gavin could be hiding behind there. I'll never know if I don't check.

Grass crunches beneath my boots. I think of the knife block sitting on the counter inside the house, the thick black handle of a butcher knife jutting out of the wood. My fingers itch. I should have thought to grab a weapon. I should have thought to call the police on the house phone.

I lower my hand to the hood of Elijah's car, kneeling as I creep around. The gravel driveway feels loose beneath the thick soles of my combat boots. Like it could crumble out from beneath me at any moment. I hold my breath, moving one foot in front of the other. Listening.

Something rustles in the darkness, and the hair on the back of my neck stands straight up. I clench and unclench my fist, wishing—again—that I'd thought to grab a knife. But Gavin wouldn't hurt me. He's creepy, not violent.

I swallow. *I hope.*

Steeling myself, I duck around to the other side of the car. Two shiny white eyes stare back at me.

I choke back a scream, and the animal—whatever it is—scurries beneath the car's front tire. I stand, my heart still pounding.

A light flashes in the trees.

"Elijah?" I take two stumbling steps toward the light, but it flickers out before I reach the tree line.

He just turned the phone off, I tell myself. Everything's fine. But my palms have started to sweat. My combat boots feel heavy. It's fine. Elijah's fine.

But Gavin is in the woods with him. Gavin is running through the dark, and Elijah doesn't know he's there. Gavin could find a tree branch or a rock. Gavin could—

I stumble, and a branch slices my bare leg, leaving my skin stinging. I push myself up again and keep going.

"Elijah!" I call. I start to run. My boots weigh me down as I thrash through the trees, but I push myself faster. "Elijah!"

The wind picks up, stealing my voice and sending the branches above me trembling. Dead leaves rain from the sky. My phone flashlight hasn't turned on again. What if he's—

Oh God.

I imagine Gavin tiptoeing through the brush. Kneeling to find a rock on the forest floor. His fingers curl around its jagged edges. He pulls his arm back, aiming. The image is so real. I can almost hear the wet thud of the rock smacking into the back of Elijah's head, breaking open his skull. I can practically smell the blood.

I push myself faster. I'm losing steam. My muscles have started to ache, and my breath comes hot and fast. I can't keep running, but I can't stop, either. Not until I find him. *Them.*

Something small darts in front of me. I jerk away from it, and my ankle twists. Suddenly I'm on the ground, pain shooting up my back, my breath coming in gasps and spurts. I squeeze my eyes shut, and a tear leaks onto my cheek.

"Shit!" I smack the ground, and a rock digs into my palm. I roll onto my side and attempt to push myself to my feet. My tailbone feels bruised. A dull ache beats through the base of my spine, like a second heart, making every movement agony. I pull one knee under me, and then the other. My ankle doesn't feel so hot. It's like the bones that hold my foot to my leg have come loose. I can practically feel them rolling around beneath my skin.

I think of the sound of bones crunching. How long has it been since I've seen the light from the phone? Two minutes? Ten?

I'm kneeling, and then I'm standing, my legs unsteady. I lurch forward, grasping for a tree branch to keep myself upright.

Movement flickers at the corner of my eye. I curl my fingers around the branch and stumble around in a slow circle, scanning the woods. "Hello?" I call. "Is someone out there?"

Nobody answers. The darkness seems like a solid thing, like something I could reach out and touch. I glance behind me and then ahead. Every direction looks the same. I have no idea which way leads back to the house and which leads deeper into the woods. I'm lost.

Part of me wants to give up. Sink to the ground and curl into a ball and wait until someone finds me. But then I think of Gavin and the way he disappeared into the darkness after Elijah, like a predator chasing down his next meal. I can't leave Elijah to deal with him alone.

I take a small step. My ankle twinges, but it doesn't collapse. I'm afraid to let go of the tree branch, but I make myself release my fingers, one by one, until I'm standing on my own. There. That's not so bad. I shuffle into the darkness, barely lifting my feet from the ground. My ankle feels almost okay. Hurt, but not broken. Pain hums below the surface of my skin, but I can handle it.

I try a bigger step, and I don't fall. I'm still not sure if I'm headed in the right direction, but at least I can walk. Cold air tickles my legs. Dead leaves shuffle beneath my shoes. After a few minutes of wandering through the dark, I hear something.

Voices.

I don't know whether to be terrified or relieved. I walk faster, ignoring the pain twisting through my leg. A light flashes in the darkness. Like a beacon.

Elijah, I think, and a desperate grin tugs at my lips. The voices sound closer. I can almost hear what they're saying.

"Please," a deep, trembling voice begs, *"I didn't—"*

"Shut up," someone else says, cutting him off.

The smile slips from my lips. They're fighting. I push past a tree branch and stumble into a clearing, my bad foot twisting beneath me. I trip, hands grasping desperately at the air, and I'm sure that I'm going to fall again when my fingers brush hard, cold bark. I steady myself against a tree, gasping.

A light is just ahead. It's coming from a cell phone in someone's hand, the beam aimed at the ground to illuminate a small circle of grass and dirt. Whoever holds the phone is hidden by the darkness. Gavin kneels before the figure, light bouncing off his golden curls, dark shadows stretching over his face. His expression is twisted. Terrified.

Something inside my chest goes cold.

"Please," Gavin begs, his hands held in surrender. "I'll leave, I promise. I'm sorry."

The person holding the phone shifts in place. It's too dark for me to see who it is, but I can make out the outline of a body. That's not Elijah. The cold feeling spreads. I take a step backward, and a twig snaps beneath my boot.

Gavin's eyes shift away from the shadow standing over him. Relief washes over his face.

"Brooklyn!" he screams. "Brooklyn, help me, please. She's crazy!"

I stop moving. *She?*

The person standing over Gavin turns, lifting the cell phone so its beam shines into my face. I cringe and lift both hands to shield my eyes from the sudden glare. Everything beyond the circle of light is black.

"Riley?" I call, squinting into the darkness. "Is that you?"

"Please." Gavin's voice is desperate now. He releases a ragged sob. "Run. Get help. Please."

Run. I tighten my grip on the tree branch, shuffling my feet backward as the light moves away from my face. Something bad is happening here. I blink at the sudden darkness, but I can't quite make out the silhouette of the person in front of me. Narrow shoulders. Long, dark hair threaded with silver.

"Hope?" I ask. "What are you doing here?"

Hope tilts the phone, sending its beam shining over her face. She looks paler than usual in the darkness, her eyes bright and mischievous. Like she's on the verge of laughing. Fear tickles the back of my neck.

"Hey, Brooklyn," she says, the corner of her mouth quirking into a smile. She has her back to Gavin, and I see him trying to stand. He looks injured. Why is he injured? "What—"

Gavin leaps to his feet, howling, and launches himself at Hope. He grabs her from behind, his hands clawing for her neck.

"Hope!" I shout.

Hope looks tiny beneath Gavin's bulging arms. Like a doll. I let go of my tree branch, stumbling toward them. Behind her, Gavin's face reddens with the effort of squeezing her neck, but Hope doesn't look scared. She calmly lifts her hand, her fingers closing around Gavin's arm. She wrenches his wrist downward, easily, and a sickening crack echoes through the woods.

I freeze. *No.* That's impossible.

Gavin drops to his knees again, his wrist still caught between Hope's fingers. His face crumbles.

"*Bitch*," he mumbles, his voice thick. "You . . . you broke my arm."

Hope tilts her head. The movement is strange, somehow more reptilian than human. Her eyes look oddly bright in the darkness, and it takes me a long moment to realize why. They're *glowing*. Like someone has replaced her irises with two softly burning embers.

She turns to face him and jerks her arm up. A wet, ripping sound fills the clearing. Something splatters against my cheeks. I wipe my face, and my fingers come away red. *Blood.*

"'And if your right hand causes you to sin, cut it off and throw it away,'" Hope says. "Matthew 5:30, right? Isn't that the passage you and Dad were always quoting?"

She tosses something to the ground in front of me. Static fills my ears, and it's a second before I realize it's not static—it's screaming. Gavin is screaming. He clutches his arm to his chest, kicking the heels of his feet into the ground like a child having a tantrum. His face is beet-red with rage. I look down.

Gavin's hand lies in the grass. It ends just below the wrist, the skin torn and bloody. Two jagged white bones jut out of the stump. Blood and meat and tissue ooze around the ligaments, seeping into the cold dirt.

CHAPTER TWENTY-FIVE

The noises Gavin makes don't sound human. He wails and shrieks, his body jerking like there's an electric pulse ripping through his muscles.

People shouldn't sound like that. They shouldn't *move* like that. I feel like I'm watching something that shouldn't be real.

His hand lies on the ground a few feet from where I'm standing. I don't look at it, but I *feel* it there, just outside my field of vision. It's a pale blur at the corner of my eye. My brain keeps trying to skip over the realness of it, but I can still hear the wet rip of Gavin's hand separating from his arm. I can still smell the blood.

My stomach turns. I used to hold that hand. Those fingers traced the lines of my face. Now they just lie there, bones broken, skin torn. I need to get out of here. I need to find Elijah.

Hope starts to laugh. It's the same light, tinkling laugh as when she giggled at Gavin's jokes during band practice.

"What *are* you?" I demand.

"I'm the pastor's daughter." Hope lifts her hand, each finger twitching as she examines the blood slicked across her skin.

She isn't human, I realize. Small, subtle movements tip me off. The sharp tilt of her neck. The red glow in her eyes. The way her hands move too quickly, like they don't need to consult her brain before acting.

She licks the blood away from her palm, smearing it across her mouth and chin. It looks black in the darkness.

"Mmm," she moans, pressing her lips together. "Tastes like sin."

I dig my fingers into the cold, rough bark behind me. I need to run. Elijah can't be far. We'll take his car and get the hell out of here. That's the only way we can get out of this alive. I shift more weight onto my injured ankle, and pain spasms up my leg. *Shit.* Tears spring to the corners of my eyes.

"You're *sick*," Gavin spits between wails, drawing my attention back to where he's crouched on the ground.

Even if I could run, I can't exactly leave him here to die alone. Snot runs down his cheeks, and his skin has turned a deep, blotchy red. "Just like Dad said. You're—"

Gavin stops talking and his eyes widen, just a little. At first it seems like he has something caught in his throat. He claws at his neck with his remaining hand, his fingernails leaving long, thin scratches on his skin.

"What are you doing to him?" I choke out, watching his face darken to a deep maroon. The color of a bruise.

"Gavin needs to be punished." Hope tilts her head even further. It's not natural. Not human. "Do you remember all those nights you listened to me scream, dear brother? All those times I asked you for help, and you told me to repent?"

A single drop of blood trickles out of Gavin's nose. It slips over his lips and clings to his chin for a fraction of a second before dropping to the grass below. Gavin stares down at the shiny red spot. He looks back up at Hope, moving his mouth like he's trying to speak.

A bubble of blood forms on his lips and then pops, spraying his face with red.

"Don't do this." I slide one foot away from the tree, ignoring the instant wave of pain that crashes over me. Gavin's face is practically purple. I can't look at him, can't watch this. "Please. Just stop."

"You're the one who told me the father and son needed to be punished for what they did to me, Brooklyn."

250

"Not like this." I let go of the tree branch, moving all my weight to my legs. My chest gets tight. My head, dizzy. I have to remind myself to inhale. Elijah has to have heard all this screaming. Maybe he's close.

If I'm going to run, I need to do it now, while Hope's distracted. But I can't look away from Gavin. I clench and unclench my hands, trying to find the strength.

Gavin keels to his side. Blood pours from the corners of his eyes, and his nose, and his mouth. His skin looks purple, and his eyes are bloodshot and so engorged that they look too big for his skull.

"Please. Help . . . me . . . ," he chokes out, his eyes finding me in the dark. Hope kneels on the ground in front of him, clicking her tongue.

"When I cried for help, you put your headphones on so you couldn't hear me," Hope says. "I don't have any headphones out here, so I'm going to have to improvise."

Hope lifts a hand, and Gavin's mouth springs open. He sticks out his tongue.

"Hope," I whisper, horrified. "Don't—"

Her fingers twitch like spider's legs. Gavin's eyes grow even wider. They bug out of their sockets like something from a cartoon. He tries to scream, but before he can make a sound, his tongue splits into two.

I throw both hands over my mouth, all thoughts of running away instantly forgotten. Gavin opens and closes his mouth, his remaining hand groping for his ruined tongue. His blond hair is streaked with blood and sweat. Those blue eyes shot through with panic. I stare, my mouth frozen in a scream. But no more sound climbs up my throat. No tears form in my eyes. I feel like I'm watching this moment from far away. Like I'm no longer inside of my own body.

Hope leans over Gavin, brushing the sweaty curls off his forehead. "Don't worry, we're not done yet."

As though on cue, Gavin begins to shake. Foam gathers at his lips and spills over onto his chin. Hope gives a final twitch of her hand, and his head drops to the ground and his eyes go still.

"You . . . killed him," I finally manage.

Hope swivels around so that she's facing me instead of Gavin, her knee brushing against Gavin's shoulder as she moves. "I didn't just do that for myself. He was going to come after you next. Consider it a thank-you."

I tear my eyes away from Gavin's purple, bloodstained face and split tongue. "Thank you?"

Hope holds the bright phone screen under her chin. Deep shadows collect in the grooves of her face, making her eyes look too big, her nose long and sharp, her mouth jack-o-'lantern wide. "For getting rid of my father, dummy. You have no idea how grateful I am that you had my back. I'd kill a hundred ex-boyfriends if you asked me to."

For a second I'm inside Hope's house again, standing in the hallway outside the bathroom. I smell smoke and burning skin. Pastor Joe's desperate voice echoes off the walls.

I grit my teeth together. *No.* I opened the lock. I did my part.

"Hope," I say, swallowing. "I don't know what you think happened at your house that night, but I didn't kill your father—"

Hope blinks. There's an amused glint to her black eyes. "I'm confused. Didn't you blind him and leave him alone in a burning room? What exactly did you think was going to happen?"

"He tortured me," I spit out. "He . . . he almost killed me in that creepy sinner's room."

Hope nods her head, thinking this over as mischievous light dances through her red eyes. "I get it, so two wrongs make a right?"

"That's not what I'm saying!" I slam a fist into the ground. "I only went after him because you told me to, remember? You said he was hurting you. You told me you needed help!"

"But Brooklyn, I *did* need help," Hope says. "I found Hope in South America. She was this sweet, angelic little girl who was just starting to realize she didn't want to be so sweet and angelic anymore."

The voice coming out of Hope's mouth isn't the same lilting, musical voice I recognize. It's deeper. Rougher.

"By the time Gavin and dear old Dad started to realize that their precious Hope might not be so innocent anymore, it was already too late for her. By then I was having too much fun helping the youth group kids."

"Helping?" I repeat. I think of Laura slipping in the frozen yogurt shop. Derick's jaw wired shut. The prayer circle page on Christ First's website, filled with one horrible mishap after another. "*You* were the one hurting the kids at youth group?"

"Brilliant, right? A fork in the eye to keep Laura from obsessing over her own reflection. Broken jaw to keep Derick from overeating. It's funny, they all said they wanted to be saved from their sins, but none of them actually thanked me."

Puzzle pieces click into place, one after another, forming a picture in my head that I don't want to look at.

"But the bruises," I choke out. "You said he was punishing you."

Hope tilts her head to the side, her eyes widening grotesquely. Her face looks like a mask.

"He wanted to 'get the demon out of me,'" she says, using air quotes. "When he found out what was happening to those youth group kids, he got it into his head to perform an exorcism." Hope giggles, her nose wrinkling. "He didn't get that I'm *happy* like this. The demon and I are the same now. But the exorcism was starting to work. He might have actually saved Hope if you hadn't burned him alive."

"But he *hurt* me," I say. "He tortured me."

"*Think.* Was he hurting you? Or was he trying to save you, like he tried to save Hope?"

I go quiet, replaying that night in my mind. Pastor Joe tied me to a chair in Hope's bedroom. He threatened me with that deadly looking angel's wing and locked me inside Hope's closet—the sinner's room. He let me bleed and cry. He nearly drowned me.

But didn't he also say he was trying to help? *You're just like Hope*, he'd said. *You need me to guide you off the path of evil.*

His voice disappears, replaced with Gavin's: *She manipulates people . . .*

"No," I whisper, almost to myself. "You're wrong. He was wrong."

"There's evil inside of you," Hope continues. "I could feel it when I called you at the helpline. It's why I finally told you about my horrible, violent father and terrible brother. I could have killed him myself, of course. But it was better that you did it."

I pull my leg beneath me and grab for a low-hanging branch to help me stand. My ankle is sore, but it holds. "Why does it matter that I did it?"

"Before you killed my father, you just had the potential for evil. It hummed inside of you, whispering for you to do terrible things. Steal a tube of lipstick, for instance. That kind of sin is powerful, but it can't take hold of your soul until you commit a truly evil act. Now that you have, the evil lives inside of you. Just like me."

The branch snaps beneath my fingers, and I crash back to the ground. I bring my knee to my chest, cringing. "I'm not evil," I say. "You're lying."

Hope just smiles. It's the same shy, innocent smile she wore when we first met. "There's no use fighting it," she says. "You killed a man. There's no turning back now. The devil has your soul."

CHAPTER TWENTY-SIX

It starts to rain. Cold drops prick my wrists and the top of my head. Wind rustles the tree branches above me, sending a fresh layer of dead leaves into the clearing. Their falling shadows look like small, winged animals.

Hope sits on the ground, legs crossed, like we're about to paint each other's nails. She watches me with her head cocked. Waiting.

You killed a man. The devil has your soul.

I close my eyes, pressing my lips together to hold back a sob. *I didn't kill him*, I want to scream. I didn't unlock the door right away, but that doesn't mean his death was my fault. He deserved what he got. I dig my fingernails into my thighs to stop my hands from shaking.

Evil should be punished. Sometimes, two wrongs do make a right.

The smell of blood hangs in the air, reminding me that my ex-boyfriend lies dead just a few feet from where I'm sitting. And my new boyfriend is still wandering around in the woods somewhere.

Hope is dangerous. I have to find Elijah and get him the hell away from her.

I move my legs under my body, using the low branch again to pull myself into a crouch.

Hope smiles. I can't see her face in the darkness, but her phone casts light on the edge of her mouth, a slightly uplifted corner of lips. "You can't run away from this," she says. "The evil is already inside of you."

Every one of my muscles tenses. I grit my teeth. "You're lying."

"Don't be an idiot. Look around."

I hesitate, still crouching. The woods are black and still, the darkness so complete it seems to pulse. Other than the tiny beam of light emitting from Hope's phone, there's nothing to see.

The rain comes down harder, soaking through my sweater and jeans. It transforms the ground into a muddy swamp beneath my combat boots. I hold tightly to the tree branch. The bark grows slick beneath my fingers, making it harder to keep my grip.

"What am I supposed to be looking at?" I ask.

Hope doesn't answer. Lightning appears in the sky above me, a jagged white cut against the black. It crashes into the tree I'm leaning against, raining sparks into the clearing. All at once the night is filled with light. And I see—

Blood. It's everywhere. It rains from the sky instead of water. It mixes with the dirt to create thick, red-tinted mud that smells like copper and death. It traces lines down Hope's cheeks and soaks through her clothes. It stains my arms and drips from my hair.

I stand, shakily, swatting at myself like the blood is something I can wipe off with my hands. But there's too much of it. I'll never get it all. The lightning dies, plunging us back into darkness. I can't see the blood anymore, but I feel it. Heavier than water. Sticky. Its overpowering scent crawling up my nostrils, making me dizzy.

"Let the evil in," Hope says. "It's easy. There's no use fighting."

I ignore her. *It's just blood*, I think, giddy with fear. There's no reason to freak out. It'll probably disappear, like the blood that came out of the shower. I just need to get away from here. Find Elijah. Get back to the car.

I take a step into the trees, my ankle still tingling with pain. I expect Hope to stand and grab me—to chase me. But she stays still, watching me like I'm a small animal. Something easily crushed.

I take another step into the woods, and another. Rain lashes at my neck and my shoulders. Only it's not rain. It slides down the back of my sweater and sloshes around inside my boots, making my socks bunch between my toes. Vomit rises in my throat, but I choke it back down. If I hold my breath, I can pretend the rain is still water. Fresh, clean water.

Wind howls through the trees. Tree branches rattle. I shiver and curl my arms around my chest. The wind picks up, and for a moment I can almost make out words. Quiet, raspy words. Like someone whispering.

Evil. Evil.

"Elijah!" I shout, my voice trembling. My leg slips out from under me, and I crash down to my knee, cringing at the pain zigzagging up my shin. Wind pushes against me. It caresses the back of my neck and tickles my ears. "Elijah! Where are you?"

Evil, the wind whispers. A breeze moves down my arm, and it feels just like a person tracing the skin between my elbow and wrist with their finger. I shriek and swat at it, but my hand touches nothing but air. The wind seems to laugh.

Evil, it says again.

I throw my hands over my ears. Hope is doing all of this. She wants to scare me, but I'm not going to let her. I push myself back to my feet and move deeper into the woods. When I'm sure that my ankle will hold, I break into a slow, sloping run.

Get to the house, I tell myself. *Find Elijah. Call the police.* Just three things. I can do three things. I push myself faster, ignoring the spasm in my ankle.

Only I'm not sure which direction leads back to the house. The woods all look the same. I could be running deeper into the trees, farther from safety. It'll be so easy for Hope to take me out when I'm exhausted and lost. Maybe that's why she isn't chasing me. She knows I'll never make it back.

Doubt gnaws at me, and I slow to a walk, panting. The woods seem to spin. I don't see any sign of Elijah. Everything looks familiar but strange. I spot a thin, spindly tree with knobby branches that I'm sure I saw a few minutes ago. I run a hand back through my hair, trying to think.

A light flashes in the darkness.

Elijah, I think, my heart pounding. I push through the trees, my breath coming fast and hot. I no longer feel the pain in my ankle or the mud slipping beneath my feet. Elijah will help me. The light glimmers in the distance like a firefly. I can't tell if it's moving or standing still.

My heart pounds, and the muscles in my legs start to feel weak. The light is just through a thicket of trees. And then it's over another hill. It's around a bend in the path. It never gets any closer.

"No," I whisper. I double over, my hands propped against my knees. It's just another trick, like the bloody rain and the whispering wind. Frustration bubbles up inside of me. I release an angry yell and kick at a pile of dead leaves. I'm running in circles.

Something thrashes through the brush behind me. I whirl around, my hands clenched into fists at my sides.

"Who's there?" I shout. The woods are dark. Silent. Fear slides through my ribs like a knife, but I'm not going to back down. I turn in a slow circle, studying every shadow between the trees, every branch and leaf swaying in the wind.

Another crack of lightning breaks the sky open and sends light flashing through the woods. Pastor Joe stands in the trees directly before me, reaching out with one crooked, blackened hand. His skin seems to be melting off his face. Black flesh drips down, mingling with blood and yellowish pus. He stumbles through the woods. Moaning.

I scream, throwing both hands over my mouth. I stumble backward, slamming into a tree.

"Evil . . . evil . . ." His voice sounds almost exactly like the raspy, whispering wind.

"You're not real," I say, out loud.

Pastor Joe's lipless mouth spreads wide, displaying two rows of cracked, yellowed teeth. I think he's smiling.

"Evil," he says again.

Get to the house, I remind myself. *Find Elijah.* I push myself away from the tree, bracing to run. Pastor Joe lumbers toward me.

"Evil . . ."

I dart forward, trying to weave my way around Pastor Joe, but he's faster than he looks. He grabs me by the shoulders and slams my body against a tree. His black, sooty fingers tighten around my arms. Wet hair falls over my forehead, and pain pounds through my spine. Pastor Joe leans closer, his skin reeking of death and smoke. I cringe and squeeze my eyes shut. I feel his breath on my cheek and then—

Nothing happens. Pastor Joe stops moaning. His fingers release from my arm. The air tickling my face is just a breeze—not breath. I open my eyes, and Pastor Joe isn't there anymore. I'm alone again.

I push myself away from the tree, certain this must be another trick. He's going to pop out from behind a bush. He's going to materialize in the darkness. I kneel, my fingers clawing along the forest floor until they locate a thick, heavy branch. I stand, holding the branch out in front of me.

"I know you're still there!" I shout. Wind rattles the leaves. Rain taps the ground. No one says a word.

I don't know how long I wander through the trees, shouting for Elijah. Rain hits my shoulders and plasters my hair against the back of my neck. The tree branch is heavy and so wet that bits of bark keep coming off in my fingers, but I refuse to put it down. I keep waiting for Pastor Joe to step out from behind a tree. I listen for the sound of footsteps or rustling leaves. But all I hear is rain.

A house emerges beyond the trees. My chest clenches. I push myself to move faster, my feet tripping over twigs and rocks. I'm still running when I realize it's too small to be the lake house. It's just a shed.

I slow to a walk. Even in the darkness I can see that it's ancient. The earthy, rotten smell of the wood fills the air, and a corner of the roof seems to have caved in. I yank the door open and duck inside. It's musty, but dry.

I close the door and rest my head against the wood to catch my breath. It's bigger on the inside than it looks on the outside. Almost the size of a one-car garage. An old lawn mower sits in the far corner, a bag half full of dead leaves slouched beside it. Ancient garden equipment hangs from the walls, the shapes foreign and mysterious in the dark. I lift my head, studying the equipment. There must be something sharp up there. A weapon.

I take a step toward the wall and trip over something lying across the floor. I glance down.

It's Gavin. Gavin, who I just ran away from. Gavin, who should be lying in the trees far, far behind me.

Blood streams from his eyes and nostrils and the corners of his mouth. His skin is so red it looks almost purple.

"No," I whisper, shaking my head. "You aren't here. You can't be here."

The door behind me blows open, crashing against the shed wall. I scream and stagger backward, nearly tripping over Gavin's dead body again.

Hope steps into the shed, a sympathetic look on her face. She purses her lips, pulling the door closed behind her. "I told you that you couldn't run away from this."

A floorboard creaks behind me. I imagine Gavin sitting up, reaching for me, and I flinch and look over my shoulder. But he's still lying on the ground. Still dead.

No. This can't be happening. I ran away from Hope. I ran and I ran. How is she here?

Anger rises in my chest, blocking out my fear and horror. It was all a trick. Hope knew I wouldn't be able to run away. I take a step toward her, my hands tightening into fists at my sides.

"You brought me here," I say. Hope tilts her head, considering me.

"What if I did?" she asks, sweetly. "What are you going to do about it?"

I want to scream. I want to hit something. I grab Hope, tightening my fingers around her throat. I can feel her heartbeat beneath my hands. Light and fluttering.

"You going to kill me, Brooklyn?" Hope asks, her voice strained. I tighten my grip. I don't want to hurt her, exactly—just shut her up. But she makes a choking sound, and her eyes roll back in her head. Her blood pumps quick and hot beneath her skin. She grabs for my arms, her body going weak. Her legs crumple beneath her, and I'm only holding her up by the neck now. I kneel, letting her body fall onto the shed floor.

It feels *good*, holding her life in my hands like this. Being the one to decide whether she lives or dies. I tighten my grip and her neck collapses beneath my fingers, like it's made of paper. She smiles, egging me on.

The anger inside of me grows hotter. Stronger. This is her fault. She said it herself—she wanted me to kill her father.

Hope breaks away from me, gasping. She tries to laugh, but her smile doesn't reach her eyes. She touches the reddened skin at her neck. "You had me worried for a second—"

I ball my hand into a fist and smack it into her face. Pain explodes against my knuckles, but it feels good. Righteous. Hope's head snaps backward. I hit her again. She drops her phone, sending the eerie, white beam shining up at the shed ceiling. She falls backward, her head hitting the floor. I climb on top of her and keep hitting. All I feel is the fire in my chest and the hot, bright pain in my hand.

She has to be destroyed, I think, punching her again. Hope tries to raise her hands, but they drop back to her sides. I feel teeth break beneath my knuckles. I feel lips split and skin tear.

Hope stops blinking.

Stops breathing.

Stops moving.

CHAPTER TWENTY-SEVEN

I sit back on my heels. Panting. My knuckles sting. I glance down at my hands, but they don't look like hands anymore, and it takes me a moment to understand what I'm seeing. Shredded skin peels away from my fingers. Bone glares up from beneath it, white and haunting in the darkness. Blood seeps into the creases around my broken nails, making them look black.

I look from my hands to Hope, still lying on the floor before me. Her teeth are broken, and her face has caved in—I must have cracked a few bones in her cheek when I was hitting her. A cut splits her lower lip, and fresh blood oozes out of it.

Nausea fills my stomach. *I did that.* My hands start to shake, so I curl them into fists. I beat a girl to death with these hands. She screamed and cried and tried to stop me, but I kept hitting her. I hit her until she went still.

I push myself to my feet. My knees knock together, and there's a second when I'm sure I'm going to drop back to the ground next to the girl I just murdered. I'm almost upset when my legs hold steady. The floor is where I belong.

I turn. Gavin is still lying on the floor of the shed, his skin purple, his split tongue dangling from his mouth. He looks like a Halloween mask, not a real person.

I keel over, vomiting, one hand propped against the wall to hold myself steady. The vomit is all watery, and it tastes like acid, but I don't stop until my insides feel raw. Everything hurts, but that's how it's supposed to be, right? I just killed a girl. I *should* hurt.

She was evil, my brain shouts. I wipe my mouth with the back of my hand, letting the words seep in. *You had to kill her. You had to stop her.*

The shed door creaks. I look up, nerves buzzing. Elijah stands in the doorway. He looks at Hope's beaten body, and then his eyes shift to Gavin's grotesque, ruined face. He lifts a hand to his mouth.

"Oh my god," he murmurs.

"No." I stumble toward him. "It's not—"

Elijah glances back at me, his eyes falling on my hands instead of my face. The space between his eyebrows creases as he sees the blood crusted around my fingernails, the skin peeling away from my knuckles.

He backs out of the shed, shaking his head. "You're . . . sick."

He says it like he can't believe it himself. Like he can't believe *anyone* would do something so horrible.

I stumble toward him. "Let me explain."

He turns and starts to run.

Shit. I push off after him, my boots slipping on the blood covering the shed's wooden floor. My mind goes blank, and all I think about is catching him. I *have* to catch him.

I expect my knees to shake and my ankle to twinge with pain, but my legs are steady beneath me. I feel strong for the first time all night. I run faster, my arms pumping at my sides.

Elijah is a shadow flitting through the trees, his dark T-shirt making it easy for him to blend into the night. His legs are longer than mine, and all that biking has left his body strong and athletic. He's going to get away. Desperation makes my chest tight. I run faster.

He seems to know where he's going. He easily leads me under trees and around scraggly bushes. He leaps over fallen logs, his legs lean coils of muscle. The ground beneath us becomes springy and soft, the mud thick with moisture. We must be nearing the lake.

I keep waiting for the distance between us to stretch. For Elijah to pull ahead and leave me running through the trees alone. But it's the opposite. *I'm* gaining on *him*. He glances over his shoulder, panting, and his eyes widen when he sees how close I've gotten. He speeds up, then stumbles on a fallen tree branch. He rights himself quickly, but now I'm only a few steps behind. I reach out, my fingers grazing the back of his shirt.

"Elijah!"

He leaps away from me, bursting through the trees. The glassy, black surface of the water appears between the branches. I was wrong, he must not know where he's going, because he skids to a stop, swearing loudly. I stumble out of the trees after him, and that's when I see his mistake. The lake stretches ahead, the woods behind. Riley's house sits farther up the hill to his right, and there's a thin stretch of land between the trees and the water leading to it—but he'll have to get past me first. He's blocked in.

He turns, his eyes shifting from me to the house behind me. I see him calculating the distance, wondering if he can make it. He bends his legs, poised to run.

I hold up both hands to show I'm not a threat. "Please stop running. I'm not going to hurt you. I just want to talk."

"Like you were talking to that girl?" Elijah asks.

"I can explain."

Elijah shakes his head, backing away from me. Water sloshes around his shoes, but he doesn't even glance down.

"I saw you hitting her," he says, breathless. "Explain that."

"It wasn't what it looked like, I swear."

Elijah stumbles farther into the lake, still gasping. He's exhausted from the run—he looks like he can barely stand. I'm not even winded.

Elijah notices this at the same moment I do. He narrows his eyes. "What's wrong with you?"

"Nothing," I say. But he's right. Something feels wrong. I shouldn't be this strong. I shouldn't have caught up to him so quickly.

The water is up to his knees now, soaking through his jeans. He has nowhere to go.

"Listen," I say. "That girl, Hope, she was—"

Elijah pulls something out of his pocket. My cell phone. "You can tell it to the cops," he says.

I leap into the water, but Elijah darts out of my way before I grab hold of him. My boots slide through the mud, and I go down. Lake water fills my nose and mouth. It soaks my clothes, leaving me cold and heavy. I push myself to my knees, but Elijah's already out of the water. He's racing away from me, stumbling into the yard surrounding Riley's house.

Shit. I stand and start to run. The muddy ground and twigs beneath me transform into well-manicured grass. Lamplight winks from behind the house's windows.

Elijah is halfway to the door. I push my legs harder, panting. I'm only three feet behind him now. Two feet. *One.* He reaches for the door—

I jump, wrapping my arms around his shoulders. He releases a grunt, and the two of us hit the ground, rolling over each other into the grass. Rocks bite into my legs, tearing through my jeans, and twigs pull at my sweater. Elijah tries to push me off, but he can't. I roll him onto his back and climb onto his chest, pressing his arms into the grass above his head. I dig my knees into the ground on either side of his torso.

"Wait," I say, gasping. "She was evil. That's what I've been trying to tell you. She killed Gavin. She—"

"Get off me, psycho." Elijah pushes against my arms, but he can't break my grip. I hold him down. Easily. He wriggles, trying again to knock me off. "How are you so strong?"

I hold both his arms down with one hand and cover his mouth with the other. "Just stop struggling for a second."

Elijah bites my fingers, but the pain doesn't bother me. It flickers and fades, like a paper cut. I push my hand harder into his mouth, grinding his teeth against my knuckles.

"Stop!" I say. "You're not listening."

Elijah wrenches an arm free and grabs for my face, his fingers clawing at my eyes and mouth. He digs his nails into my cheeks, like my skin is a mask he can rip off. I take my hand off his mouth and grab him by the wrist, pulling his arm away from my face.

"Let me go!" he shouts. "You fucking freak."

"Shut up!" I cover his mouth with my hand again. He keeps grabbing for my face, so I shift my knee, pinning his elbow in the dirt. He stares at me with wide, terrified eyes. There's no kindness in those eyes. He doesn't believe a word I'm saying.

Why doesn't he believe me?

I squeeze my own eyes shut. Tears gather beneath my closed lids, and I hate myself for them. I'm not going to cry. *Shit*, I just need to think, and I can't do that with Elijah staring at me like I'm some disgusting *thing*. There's still a way for both of us to be okay. He just needs to fucking *listen*. Why can't he do that?

"Please," I whisper, and Elijah bucks beneath me. I dig my knees into the dirt, gripping his body tighter. He writhes and squirms. I'm just making it worse by holding him down. He's never going to believe me now.

Think, damn it! I blink, somehow managing to keep my tears at bay. If I let Elijah go, he'll tell the police that I'm a killer. I'll go to jail.

That is so messed up. I can't go to jail. What I did to Hope was *necessary*. She was evil, and I stopped her. It was hard and it was messy, but it was the right thing to do. If Elijah would just listen, he would understand that. I could make him understand.

Elijah twists his head to the left, and then to the right, trying to shake my hand from his mouth. I curl my fingers around the side of his face to hold him steady.

"Hold still," I beg. His face feels fragile in my hand. Like a baby bird. My brain screams at me to hit him. To *make* him listen. But all I want to do is curl up in his arms. I want him to hold me and tell me that everything will be all right.

A tear rolls down my face and hits Elijah's cheek. He cringes.

The tears keep coming. Elijah used to care about me. All those feelings couldn't have just gone away.

"She was evil," I whisper again, my voice trembling. "I didn't want to hurt her, I swear."

He goes still beneath me.

"Elijah?" I push the hair off his sweaty forehead, my hand shaking. "You believe me, don't you?"

His eyes soften. I move my hand from his mouth, and this time, he doesn't scream or shout. He blinks and licks his lips. Hope flickers inside of me.

"You have to believe me," I whisper, kissing him on

the cheek. The tears keep rolling down my face, but it's okay now. It's all going to be okay. The tension leaves Elijah's shoulders and arms. I let go of his wrist and move my knee off his elbow so he can pull me closer. "I knew you would believe me. I knew it."

Elijah releases an angry growl and hurls his body forward. I lose my balance, rolling off him and hitting the ground—*hard*. For a moment, I can't breathe.

Hurt like I've never felt before spreads through my body. He's never going to believe me. Part of me wants to die, right here. Close my eyes and never open them again. An itchy, gnawing feeling grows inside of my chest. It's like there's something inside of me, fighting to get out.

Elijah scrambles to his hands and knees, clawing up chunks of dirt and grass as he tries to push himself to his feet.

I reach out and grab him around the ankle—then jerk him back down.

He slams to the ground face-first, his head snapping into the dirt. I hear a dull thud. Then silence.

"Elijah?" I crawl forward and roll him onto his back. A deep, twisted cut splits his forehead. He must've hit a rock. Skin peels back from his skull, blood bubbling up beneath it. The area has already started to swell. I touch the edge of the wound, gently, with my fingertips. Blood rushes out of it, quickly covering Elijah's face and my fingers. His eyes can't quite focus on mine.

"What—" He starts to raise a hand, then drops it again. The blood spreads, dripping from his skin and soaking into the grass and dirt beneath him. It pools under his head, spreading beneath my knees. I jostle Elijah's arm.

"Wake up," I say, my voice small. I didn't mean to hurt him. I just wanted to keep him from running away. I just wanted him to *listen*. "Please wake up. *Please.*"

Elijah's eyes shift, and for a second, I think he's trying to look at me. Then they go still. I watch him for a long moment, waiting for him to blink or twitch or move. But he doesn't. He's gone.

"No," I whisper. My chest is hot and sticky. It feels like there's something gnawing at the inside of my skin. Hope and Pastor Joe had it coming. But Elijah didn't do anything wrong. He was innocent.

I close my eyes, dropping my forehead against his. Blood pools between our faces. I did this to him. There's no going back now.

You're evil, Hope told me.

She was right.

CHAPTER TWENTY-EIGHT

Eventually, I stand. My legs are stiff, my jeans crusted with dirt and blood. Elijah is still holding my cell phone. It lights up with a text, but the screen is too smeared with bloody fingerprints for me to make out what it says or who it's from. I lean over and pry the phone from his fingers. They've already started to go cold.

The lake house looms ahead, the windows all lit up in the darkness. I stumble across the yard and up the two concrete stairs and into the house. I push the door closed with two hands and lean my head against the wood. The wind howls outside, but it no longer sounds like it's whispering. It's just wind.

I close my eyes and take two long, deep breaths. Then I look down at the cell phone in my hand. I dial three numbers and hit send. I try not to think about the blood coating the screen as I lift the phone to my ear.

A woman's curt voice answers, a Mississippi accent making her vowels long. "911, what's your emergency?"

I suck a breath in through my teeth. "My boyfriend is . . . hurt. Please come."

I recite the lake house address from memory and end the call before the operator can ask me any more questions. There will be plenty of questions later. Right now, I need time to think.

I go back outside and sit on one of the wooden Adirondack chairs on the patio. It's cold, but it's not raining anymore. Wind moves over the lake, sending ripples across the black surface of the water. I don't even shiver.

Elijah lies on the ground a few feet away, staring up at the black sky. I keep waiting for him to blink, or twitch, or sit up, but he doesn't move. Blood drips from the cut on his forehead and pools beneath his hair.

I don't know how long I sit there before I hear the siren and see red and blue lights flashing in the trees. An ambulance races up the drive, a sleek, black car following close behind it. I shield my eyes with one hand, squinting. I recognize that car. The police must've called Riley's parents to alert them of a crime on their property.

I bring my knees to my chest and wrap my arms around my legs. The ambulance pulls to a stop, rocks crunching beneath its thick tires. People wearing blue uniforms leap from the back, pulling a stretcher between them. They see Elijah's body lying in the grass before they spot me curled in my chair on the patio, and they race over to him. The lights are too bright. I cringe, trying not to look at them directly.

Another car door slams open and shut. I squint into the darkness beyond the flashing ambulance lights as a shadow moves down the path toward the house. I don't recognize Riley until she ducks around the ambulance.

"Brooklyn?" she calls. She looks like a Barbie doll that someone's dressed up for a slumber party, in her pink polka-dotted pajamas, her hair swept back in a matching headband. She's even wearing slippers—fuzzy ones. She wraps her arms across her chest and glances at the EMTs, but they're still crouched around Elijah. "What are you doing here?"

"There was an accident," I say, in a hollow voice.

Riley can't seem to figure out how to react. She opens her mouth and then closes it again. The skin between her eyebrows crinkles. She half-turns, watching the EMTs work behind her. They're loading Elijah onto the stretcher, barking orders at each other as they lift his body from the ground. There's so much blood. It's on their uniforms and the stretcher. It covers Elijah's face.

I didn't realize a human head held so much blood.

Riley brings her hand to her mouth, her fingertips lightly grazing her bottom lip. "Who—"

"DOA," an EMT shouts, cutting her off.

Riley sinks into the chair beside me. "DOA?" she says, almost to herself. Her eyes flick back over to me. "That . . . that means he's dead, right?"

I nod.

"Oh God," she murmurs, covering her mouth with both hands. She tucks her fuzzy-slippered feet beneath her chair and starts to rock in place. It reminds me of when we were little and used to sleep over at each other's house. She used to rock like that when she woke up from bad dreams. "What happened?" she asks, voice cracking. "Who did this? Who *was* that?"

The story I've been practicing flashes into my head. I open my mouth, and for a second nothing comes out. I could still tell the truth. Riley might even believe me.

I study her face, trying to imagine her reaction. Her skin has turned a sick greenish white. Her mouth is thin and frowning—so different from her usual calculating smile. Her chin actually trembles. She stares at me, waiting for me to explain. Waiting for me to tell her that everything will be okay.

My mouth feels suddenly dry. Elijah didn't believe me, and he actually liked me. Riley can barely stand to be around me.

"My friend . . . Elijah." I nod at the stretcher the EMTs are loading into the back of the ambulance. "He went crazy."

I say the words slowly, testing them out on my tongue. Something inside my chest begins to hum. It's like a second heartbeat, warm and steady.

It feels . . . good.

Riley's hands start to shake. "Oh my god."

"He killed Hope," I continue. "Gavin, too."

"No," Riley says, a choked sob escaping her mouth. Horror twists her features, leaving her lips curled and thin, her eyes squinting. It's the ugliest I've ever seen her.

The humming inside me grows stronger. Hotter. I feel it like a flame.

"Their bodies are in the woods," I say. "There was so much blood—"

"Stop!" Riley throws her hands over her ears. A fat tear rolls down her cheek, catching in the corner of her mouth. She squeezes her eyes shut as another tear rolls down her cheek, and another. For a long moment the only sounds between us are her muffled sobs and her voice whispering "stop" again and again.

After a moment she lowers her hands, sniffling. Her eyelashes are still heavy with tears, her eyes bloodshot. She swallows. "Why are you okay?"

I pause. "I . . . I fought him off."

Riley wipes her cheeks with the back of her hand. "But you're not even hurt. Didn't you try to help them?"

"It happened so fast." I realize that my ankle has healed, that all my cuts and bruises are gone. All that's left is dried blood—most of it not mine.

Riley's eyes move from my face to my hands, which are still clenched in my lap. I slide them beneath my thighs, but not before she notices the blood beneath my fingernails and crusted into my knuckles. She starts shaking her head, very slowly. I don't think she realizes she's doing it.

"That doesn't—" She stands suddenly, and my hand shoots out, grabbing her wrist before she can walk away.

"Where are you going?" I ask.

She glances back at me—and freezes. I don't know what she sees, but I feel the heat rising inside of me. It fills up all my dark places. It makes me powerful. Whole.

I stand, tightening my fingers around Riley's wrist. I'm taller than she is. Just by a few inches, but she still has to look up at me. She doesn't seem nearly as confident and pulled together as she does at school, dressed in her designer battle armor, surrounded by her army of mean girls. She looks small and lonely now. Just one scared little girl in the woods.

She pulls her arm away from me, and she must expect me to hold tighter, because she yanks too hard. I loosen my fingers at the right moment and she stumbles back a few steps, nearly slipping on the wet grass.

"What's wrong with you?" she asks, hugging her arm to her chest.

I tilt my head, studying her. "What are you talking about?"

She hesitates and then motions to her eyes. "There was something in your eyes. You looked . . ."

She doesn't finish her sentence. Instead, she takes another step backward.

"I'm fine," I say.

"No. You . . . you did something. You're not telling me the whole truth." She takes another slow, deliberate step away from me. "There's something wrong with you."

The humming inside of me grows louder. Warmer. It's a purring animal sitting on my chest. It's a creature made of fire and warmth.

"You're . . . you're crazy," Riley says.

My lips pull into a wide smile over my teeth. The heat inside of me flares. "Prove it," I say.

EPILOGUE

EIGHT MONTHS LATER

The new girl stands in the line ahead of me in the cafeteria, picking at the skin around her fingernail. I smell the blood on her hands before I glimpse her face. The smell is earthy, metallic. Old pennies. Fresh dirt. I tilt my head and close my eyes to breathe it in.

It reminds me of kneeling in the woods next to Elijah's body. Watching his eyes go still. My fingers twitch at the memory.

The line shuffles forward, and now the girl is grabbing a napkin and apologizing to the boy in front of her. She's harmless looking, with her thick, black curls and her innocent eyes. She wears jeans and a plain, gray

T-shirt. Like she doesn't want anyone to look at her. Like she's hiding from something.

The boy—Charlie; I recognize his rumpled polo and messy hair—says something to her, and the girl smiles. It's a shy smile, barely a twitch at the corner of her lips, but I recognize it. She's flirting. She just met Charlie and already she wants him. I can see the lust radiating in the air around her.

A drop of blood drips from her finger and hits the ground, leaving a bright red spot on the concrete. The girl doesn't seem to notice.

I tuck a lock of bleached blond hair behind one ear and tilt my head, studying her. It's not just the blood and the smile. There's something about this girl. Somewhere beneath the "don't look at me" T-shirt and the innocent eyes, she's a little wrong. I can smell it on her.

Sin. Evil.

The corner of my mouth quirks upward. This girl has a secret. A terrible, ugly little secret. And I'm going to find out what it is.

Excitement rises inside of me, and it's all I can do not to laugh out loud. I wonder if this is how Hope felt when she met me. Like the world had just handed her a terrible, wonderful gift.

I lean forward, poking the girl on the arm. A spark of static electricity stings my finger.

She turns, her dark, innocent eyes narrowing when she sees me. I catch a flash of something deep within those eyes, and I know that I'm right about her. This girl did a bad thing. She's like me. Oh, we're going to have so much fun together.

"Hey," I ask, unzipping my backpack. "Do you need a Band-Aid?"

ACKNOWLEDGMENTS

I couldn't have written this book without my extraordinary Alloy family there to hold my hand—thank you, thank you, thank you, Hayley Wagreich, Josh Bank, and Sara Shandler. You are brilliant humans. And a special thank-you to Romy Golan for looking out for my books overseas, and to Laura Barbiea for all your help on the social media front. I can't believe this is my job sometimes.

The team at Razorbill is truly amazing. I couldn't have written this book without Jessica Almon or the nonstop support I received from Casey McIntyre and Ben Schrank, Anna Jarzab, Felicia Frazier, Kristin Smith, and the rest of Razorbill's sales, marketing, and publicity team, who all worked so hard to help people discover my books. In addition to the people named here, there are so many others working behind the scenes to make this book happen. I am grateful to all of you. I couldn't have done it without your support.

And finally, thanks to my fabulous, supportive family and friends. I'm consistently blown away by all of you. I couldn't have asked for better people in my life.

And, of course, thank you to Ron, who hasn't read this book yet but will, even though it'll give him nightmares.